The King Boy

BY JUDY CAROLE RHODES

Bradbury Press • New York

Maxwell Macmillan Canada • Toronto
Maxwell Macmillan International
New York • Oxford • Singapore • Sydney

Bradbury Press
Macmillan Publishing Company
866 Third Avenue
New York, NY 10022

Maxwell Macmillan Canada, Inc.
1200 Eglinton Avenue East
Suite 200
Don Mills, Ontario M3C 3N1

Macmillan Publishing Company is part of the Maxwell Communication Group of Companies.

First edition
Printed and bound in the United States of America
10 9 8 7 6 5 4 3 2 1

Library of Congress Cataloging-in-Publication Data
Rhodes, Judy Carole.
The King Boy / by Judy Carole Rhodes. — 1st ed.
p.   cm.
Summary: Benjy's childhood in rural Arkansas is enriched by the special times he spends with his grandfather, but it is not until his grandfather's death that an old family secret is revealed.
ISBN 0-02-776115-0
[1. Grandfathers—Fiction.   2. Country life—Fiction.
3. Arkansas—Fiction.]   I. Title.
PZ7.R34763Ey   1991
[Fic]—dc20   91-2159

To you . . . who first saw the spark.
The fire is burning now. . . . Can you feel
the glow within you?

Contents

PART TWO: CHANGES

PART ONE:

Benjy's Younger Days

CHAPTER ONE

The First Day of School

If somebody would have explained to Benjy in the beginning that his schooling was going to take twelve long years, he probably would have had to been beaten and dragged the whole way. And now, at the age of sixteen, Benjy knew that was the whole idea behind keeping it a secret. Looking back on it, Benjy was only sure about one thing: starting school was the first worst day in his life.

It just didn't figure in Benjy's mind that school should be starting right when the big old bass in his Grandpa King's pond were beginning to chase everything that wiggled. And even though his momma had been preparing and warning him about this thing called school, Benjy just kept thinking that it was

1

some kind of punishment he was sure to get if he took a notion to misbehave.

His momma came into his room that first morning and began laying out a pair of new jeans and a new shirt that Benjy didn't even know he owned. Before he could get good and awake, she ripped the warm covers from his bed and said in a cheery and singing voice, "Get up, get up, you sleepy head. The sun is rising and you're still in bed." Benjy knew right then that his momma was really going to send him away to school because she had never sung him awake before, and new clothes were only for church. Benjy quickly yanked the covers back over his head, but his momma yanked right back.

"Benjy, get up! Today's your first day of school." She was still being cheery, but the singing had stopped. "I've got your clothes laid out and breakfast is ready. You can skip the morning chores today because I don't know what time that bus will be coming. Come on, now, get up. You can't be late on your first day."

Benjy was brooding as he slowly crawled out of bed and stood in the middle of his room, watching his momma as she scurried around his bed, tucking in sheets and quilts until every wrinkle was gone. When she was finished with the bed, she looked at Benjy and he knew he was next. With the same energy and determination, she began to help him dress. Finally Benjy had had all he could take. "Momma, why do I have to go to school? I've done my chores, and ain't caused you or Papa an ounce of trouble.

Why do you want to send me away to school?"

Benjy watched as his momma's face turned from cheery to just plain sad. Her eyes reminded him of his hound dog, Ole Blue, when he'd done wrong and was coming to Benjy, hoping for a little understanding. She quit fidgeting with his clothes and took a seat beside him on the bed. She ran her fingers through his hair and then softly said, "Benjy, we ain't sending you away to school because you've been bad. School's a nice place to go to so you can learn and grow up to be a smart boy."

It was the first time Benjy could remember that he really thought his mother was lying to him. How many times had his Grandpa King rubbed his head with those big, rough hands of his and said, "Benjy, you're from my own flesh and blood. Smart enough to know better, yet too young to resist." Surely if his grandpa had already seen how smart he was, then his momma was aware of it, too. Benjy frowned in an arguable way and said, "Momma, Grandpa King said I was as smart as he was, so I don't need to go to school." Momma's jaws tightened and a frown appeared on her face. Grandpa King was not one of her favorite people. So as not to set her off in a rage, Benjy quickly added, "Besides that, I'm going to be eight years old and I've already killed a deer. I do my chores good, and I've got religion. And can't nobody besides my papa and grandpa out fish me. Ain't that smart enough?"

Momma's face softened up once more. "I ain't about to argue those points with you, son. But that

3

kind of learning is what you call common sense. Me and your daddy can teach you that. The kind of learning you'll get in school is called book learning, like reading and writing and learning to count numbers."

Benjy grinned inside himself. Now he knew that his momma hadn't been lying to him. She was just trying to trick him. It was the same kind of trick he used on Ole Blue when he picked up a stick and hollered at him to fetch. Benjy would rare back to throw and when Ole Blue looked up, he'd hide the stick behind his back. Ole Blue would do tailspins, trying to figure out where that stick was. Benjy figured that his momma was just trying to get him in a tailspin about going to school. After all, there wasn't a single book in the house except the Bible, and Preacher Wilson read the Bible regularly on Sundays. Even though Benjy wasn't much on listening, he figured that later on when he grew up, he'd listen a little harder. Preacher Wilson hadn't missed a Sunday reading that Bible yet, and he wouldn't stop until he'd saved every sinner in the world. So there wasn't any need of learning to read. As for writing, Benjy wasn't quite sure of what it was. But there hadn't been any need of it so far, so there wasn't any need of worrying about it now.

And counting . . . ever since he'd been knee-high to a stump and holding a fishing pole, Benjy had been learning to count. His grandpa would say, "Hey, boy, you've got one." And there would be a fish hanging from the end of his pole. Then he'd say, "Boy, you've already caught two fish, and I ain't got a bite yet."

And sure enough, there would be two fish flopping in the bottom of the boat. Next he'd say, "All right, we got three caught now. We're going to catch a mess today." And the older Benjy got, the more fish he caught and the more numbers he learned.

He figured that once he got to school and showed everybody that he already knew what they were planning to teach him, they would just shake their heads in pure amazement and send him back home. So Benjy decided to play along with his momma.

She had set his ham and biscuits on the table before him and was smiling as she said, "Now, Benjy, that bus ain't coming to our house so I'll walk you to the county road today to make sure you catch it. But after today, you'll walk by yourself."

I'll be darn, Benjy thought to himself. They are really making this going to school hard on me. As he ate his last biscuit, he was wishing his papa was around for a man-to-man talk about how to avoid this thing called school.

His papa was as big as an oak tree and about as broad as one, too. He had coal black hair and a matching beard that he used to tickle Benjy when they wrestled. His papa was not the talking kind, and when he did talk, his voice was soft and quiet-like. Yet unlike his voice, his words were always strong and powerful in meaning. He was a showing kind of man, and even though his wife fussed at times, saying Benjy was too young, he took his son everywhere and showed him everything. When he was under the hood of his old pickup, he would have Benjy propped up there to watch. He never said anything unless Benjy asked. And it was the same way when they went hunting and fishing. He would always say, "Just watch, son. Watch and you'll learn." About the only time he ever did any explaining was just before a whipping. He never whipped Benjy when he was angry. In a voice as calm as Grandpa's pond on a hot summer day, he would explain to Benjy the wrong he had done. And until Benjy learned different, he would always think his papa was going to let him go with just a good talking to. But when he was through talking, he would stand up and pull off his worn and scarred leather belt and get his point across in another way. And when he was done, he would always say the craziest words Benjy had ever heard. "It's for your own good, boy. It hurts me worse than you, but it's for your own good."

Benjy's thinking was interrupted as his momma took his plate from the table and said, "Son, stop that daydreaming and get in there and brush your teeth and lay that cowlick down. I want you to look your best today. It's important that you make a good impression on your teachers right off the bat."

As Benjy came back into the kitchen, his momma gave him an inspecting look. Then she licked her thumb and wiped it across his cheek, as if removing a smudge. Benjy knew that it was just out of habit, because he hadn't been outside to get dirty. But he also knew better than to put up a fight, because when his momma decided to spit clean his face, no matter where he was or what he was doing, that's exactly what she did.

Benjy walked outside, just before the sun peeped over the top of the old oak trees that surrounded the house. Ole Blue came out of the barn and stopped and stretched and then stuck his rear end high into the air and his two front paws way out in front of him. He then started yawning real big and shaking his big-boned head, like he was trying to wake up. As usual, he wasn't in any hurry. The only two things that motivated Ole Blue were a deer chasing and his evening meal. The rest of the time he made the world wait for him.

Ole Blue and Benjy were born and raised together, and living off in the woods by themselves made them best of friends. Benjy watched as Ole Blue came over to him, wagging his whip of a tail. When he licked at Benjy's outstretched hand, Benjy felt lonesome about leaving him that day. He was just before kneeling down to give Ole Blue his usual good-morning bear hug when Momma appeared at the screen door, threatening him like lightning down on an oak. "Benjy, you get one speck of dirt on your knees before you get to school, and I'll whip you all the way to that bus and be waiting when you get off it to whip you all the way home." Benjy knew she meant it, too. It wasn't her fooling-around tone of voice. So he just reached down and scratched Ole Blue real good behind the ears, instead. Ole Blue sat back on his haunches and let his long pink tongue hang out one side of his mouth, as he panted in contentment. He was waiting for Benjy to slap the side of his leg and begin the day's chores. It was the only day Benjy could remember wanting to do chores, too.

Momma reappeared at the door and came out handing Benjy a sack. She looked down at his knees just to be sure she had gotten her point across. Once she was satisfied, she said, "Here's your lunch and there's a nickel in the bottom for milk. Be sure you drink it all, too. I ain't paying for something to be wasted."

Benjy let out a long sigh. Lunch in a sack, buying milk, reading, writing, counting numbers, and riding a bus were all balled up inside of him and making him as nervous as a long-tailed cat in a roomful of rocking chairs. As a last resort, to save himself from school, Benjy thought of crying. He was just before letting the tears fall when his momma said, "You know, there's a good chance that you might get to see one of those televisions we've been hearing about on the radio. I hear tell that rich folks living in the big city already have them. Your school might get one, too."

Benjy forgot about crying. Just that past Saturday night, when the family had gathered around the radio to listen to the Grand Ole Opry, they had heard about television. Papa had told Benjy that it was just like a radio, but you could see the people doing the talking and singing. Anxiously he asked, "Do you really think I'll get to see one, Momma?"

She nodded her head, sensing her son's curiosity and excitement. "Could be . . . could be. We best hurry now so you don't miss that bus."

CHAPTER TWO

The Bus Ride

Benjy completely forgot about school and asked a million questions about television as they walked to the county road. None of which his momma could answer. She let out a sigh of relief when she heard the school bus coming around blind man's curve. Even though it sounded like a logging truck, Benjy knew it had to be the bus, and once again his fear returned. All the logging trucks had already made their run to the woods at daybreak. That was his papa's business, hauling logs. He didn't own his own logging truck yet, but the family was saving for one. Sometimes late at night, Benjy would hear his papa talking about the new truck, and he would always tell his momma that things would be different then. They

9

wouldn't be poor anymore. Benjy didn't know what poor meant, but he knew it was something important because it was discussed more than once. His papa would always end those talks with, "There's better days ahead, Ruth. Things won't always be like this."

On one of Grandpa's rare visits to the house, Benjy overheard a conversation in which Grandpa offered to buy Papa a new truck. Papa refused him and an argument broke out between the two of them. Benjy was told to leave the room, and he left quickly, but only went out of sight. He knew it wasn't proper to listen in uninvited, but his desire to know what had come between his papa and grandpa was not to be denied this time. Everybody either didn't know the truth or wasn't telling it, and Benjy figured it was time to take matters into his own hands.

As Benjy listened from behind a closed door, he heard his grandpa offer to buy Papa a logging truck. His papa replied coldly, "I don't want your truck and I don't need your help."

Grandpa didn't like those words and he answered, "I understand that you're trying to hurt me and punish me, but what you don't understand is that you're hurting your family more than it hurts me. There's an awful lot I can do for you, son, if you'll just let me. There ain't no rhyme or reason why you and your family can't live a better life than this. It's yours for the taking."

By the pause in the conversation, Benjy knew that his papa was either doing some powerful thinking, or his temper was slowly rising to the boiling point. When his papa spoke again, there was a hissing sound, like he was pushing the words through his teeth. "I ain't trying to hurt you or punish you. That ain't my job. But I am an authority on things that don't seem to have no rhyme or reason to them. You made sure of that, didn't you, Daddy?"

Benjy's heart raced in anticipation of an all-out war being declared, and he knew he was closer to the truth than he had ever been. But when his grandpa spoke, it was barely a whisper, and Benjy had to strain to hear his words. "I can't change the past, boy. I'm just trying to do right by you now."

The last words spoken were "It's a little late for good intentions, Daddy, because, you see, I can't change the past, either."

The slamming of the screen door echoed through the house, and Benjy knew his grandpa was gone, along with his hopes of ever finding out the truth.

Benjy's thoughts were interrupted as he watched the bus topping the last hill. He kept hoping that bus would go on by and leave him be. But all too soon, the brakes started squealing and, amidst a cloud of dust, the big doors on the bus opened wide. His momma was fanning dust as she greeted the driver. "Good morning, sir. This is my son, Benjy, and I guess he's a little scared, this being his first day and all."

Benjy looked at the driver, who was grinning back at him, and he was overwhelmed by his size. He had always thought that his papa was a big man, but this man could make two of his papa, at least around the middle. Benjy guessed he was the type to enjoy a Sunday dinner as much as Preacher Wilson did. He had big, puffy jaws, caused by his necktie squeezing him too tight around his collar. The driver chuckled, "Don't you worry, ma'am. We'll take good care of your son." He reached in his back pocket and pulled out a handkerchief to wipe the sweat from his brow and forehead. "My name is Mr. Keeper and I'm the principal. Who might you be?"

Momma answered back, "I'm Ruth King and my husband is Joe King. He's in the logging business."

Mr. Keeper looked surprised. "Your husband is Buck King's boy, is that right?"

Benjy's momma sure didn't like it when folks related Grandpa and her husband. And she didn't mind setting somebody straight about it, whether they were friend or stranger. "I guess he is, Mr. Keeper, but the last name is all they have in common and you keep that in mind."

Mr. Keeper sensed he was stirring up a hornet's nest and he left well enough alone. He wiped his brow once more and said, "Get on, boy. We've got lots of miles to cover."

Benjy crawled on as his momma gave him a push. Ole Blue was coming up right behind him, and Benjy heard him whimper when Momma pulled him away. As the doors were closing, his momma said, "Mind your manners, Benjy." His chin began to quiver, but

12

then he looked up and saw faces peering over the top and around the corners of all the seats, and he wasn't about to cry in front of strangers.

Mr. Keeper bellowed, "Get on back and find yourself a seat, boy." Benjy sat in the first empty seat he came to, and then he looked out the window at Momma, waving with one hand and holding Ole Blue with the other. He could tell Ole Blue didn't understand this any more than he did. That's why they were such good friends. As Benjy sat there watching them, his heart was breaking. He waved back as the bus started to move away and saw his momma wiping her eyes. Then he wasn't sure whether he was coming back or not. Why else would she be crying?

Actually, he knew better. Still, that was the way he was feeling on the inside. But as soon as the bus got going good, Benjy felt his teeth hitting together and his cheeks jumping. He was having a hard time not being bounced out of his seat. Then he took a side glance over to the seat across from him. He saw two eyes staring back, and he quickly turned and looked out the window. They were just before reaching his grandpa's farm. Benjy made up his mind right then and there that if the bus stopped, he was getting off. He hadn't had a chance to discuss this schooling business with his grandpa yet, and he was needing to hear a second opinion. As the bus was passing by his grandpa's house, Benjy halfway stood up and was straining his eyes for just one glimpse of the old man. If his grandpa could see him, Benjy knew he would get him off the bus. But he wasn't there. Benjy gave a lonesome, yearning look at the farm and barely caught sight of the pond, with the sun glistening off the top of the water. He could have sworn he saw a big bass jump up and flip his tail. His grandpa was probably sitting on the bank, expecting him to be coming around soon. But he wasn't wishing it any more than Benjy was.

The pasture land seemed to stretch for miles. It always amazed Benjy that one man could own so much land, and there was one thing Benjy knew for sure: Owning it didn't make his grandpa a well-liked man. Benjy wasn't sure why that was so. Sometimes when menfolk would stop by the house for a visit, Benjy would listen in while his papa and the others would be discussing and cussing any and everything. Once he overhead an older man who worked with his papa say, "Joe, it's a wonder you turned out so good . . . you being Buck King's boy." Benjy had really strained his ears, hoping for just one hint or clue that would explain the strong disliking for his grandpa. But instead, his papa shrugged his big shoulders and answered him back, "I don't reckon I'm anything like him, and I'm proud of it, too."

One of the worst word fights Benjy could remember between his momma and papa was over his getting to visit with Grandpa King. His momma was raving about how she didn't want her son hanging around the likes of the old man for fear he'd turn out just like him. But his papa, the man of few words, laid down the law that day. He halfway raised his voice, which was the loudest Benjy had ever heard him speak. "Ruth," he said, "You know how I feel about my daddy. We sure ain't agreed on a whole lot of things in my life, but my boy is gonna know his grandpa, good or bad, just like I knew my grandpa when I was a boy. I ain't gonna turn my boy against his own kin. Benjy will make that decision when he's old enough. If he sees his grandpa as a good man, then maybe he'll be seeing something the rest of us missed. If he sees his bad side, he won't stay around him long. But either way, it will be his decision, because I ain't gonna have my boy old and grown and wondering why we never let him know his grandpa. The old man ain't got many years left, but he'll know his grandson. If I see some bad influencing going on, then maybe I'll change my mind. But as for now, this is how it will be."

The first time Benjy was allowed to go to his grandpa's place to fish, he was scared and expecting to meet with the devil himself. But it wasn't any time before they were talking and fishing like they were best of friends. His grandpa was really a sight to behold. He was a short man and skinny as a willow branch. Most of the time, he wore overalls that were a bit too big and a smart-looking Stetson hat that he was mighty proud of. But the first thing you noticed about him was not his overalls or hat. It was his eyes. They were bluer than a jaybird, and one eye had a brown spot right in the middle of the blue. When he was mad, his blue eyes were cold and hard and seemed to pierce right through you. And then the strangest thing would happen. That brown spot would grow larger and larger until it looked like he had two different-colored eyes. It was evil looking, and if you didn't know better, you would think he was a crazy man. Benjy had only seen his grandpa mad once or twice, and that was enough for him.

But those angry, scary eyes were also the same eyes that sparkled like Aunt Milly's dangling earbobs when he was happy and laughing. He was always teasing Benjy, and when he pulled one of his tricks and it worked, he would lay his head back and cackle out loud. Then his eyes danced to the sound of his own laughter.

There were also times when Benjy looked at his grandpa, and the sadness in his eyes seemed to tell a story about his past. His eyes would become cloudy and distant, and it was like he was suffering and hurting terribly on the inside. And even though Benjy didn't know the cause of his pain, he hurt for his grandpa just the same.

One time Benjy and his grandpa were out fishing, and Benjy got the nerve of a curious cat. "Grandpa," he said, "I know some of the people around here don't like you very much. Why is that?"

His grandpa just raised his pole from the water to check his hook for bait, and then chuckled a little like it didn't bother him at all. "Boy," he said, "it ain't that they don't like me. It's just that they're envious of me . . . like they want what I've got." He lowered his pole back in the water and then continued. "Your old grandpa owns darn near everything this side of the Arkansas River, and I guess that gets under a lot of people's skin when they go to thinking about what they ain't got."

At the time, the old man's explanation made perfect sense, because Benjy had experienced a strong disliking for B.J. Williams for those same reasons. One Sunday morning before church, B.J. had shown Benjy an aggie shooter that sparkled and shined like no marble he had ever seen. Benjy wanted that marble real bad, but B.J. wouldn't play it in a game for anything. And no matter how many marbles Benjy won from him, before and after church, B.J. would just pull that aggie out of his pocket and throw it up and down in the air as if to say, I still own the only one you want. And it was true, too. So for a long time, it didn't matter what other people said about his grandpa, because Benjy understood the reason they were saying it.

But there was still one part that bothered Benjy, and that was why his momma and papa felt the way they did about his grandpa. It wasn't jealousy, because he had offered to share with them when he told his papa that he would buy him a logging truck. Knowing it was the wrong thing to do, but not being able to help himself, Benjy told his momma what his grandpa had said about his reputation. He had hoped his momma would shed some new light on the subject, but instead, it just confused him more. Her face was stern and cold, and she spoke between gritted teeth. It was like she was afraid that if she opened her mouth too wide, the truth would come spilling out. And had it been left up to her, Benjy probably would have been told the truth many times over. But his papa's wishes were always respected, and all his momma said was, "Maybe folks ain't sore because of what your grandpa's got, but because of what he ain't got and how and why he lost it." And then she left the room in a fury.

When the bus started slowing down, Benjy looked out the window and saw the schoolhouse for the first time. It was a large, redbrick building with white trimming, and it sort of resembled the church, except it was much larger.

Benjy was surprised to see that he had been riding the whole time with some kids that he knew. As he watched B.J. Williams climb off the bus, Benjy was real glad he had not allowed himself to cry when he first got on. Those that knew him would have teased him for sure if he had. Benjy's insides were churning like butter as he got up and proceeded to get off the bus. He didn't have the slightest notion where he was going or what he was supposed to do. He looked up and saw Mr. Keeper staring at him through a big mirror that hung above his head. He had one eye sort of cocked and was giving Benjy the stare of a cat that was just before pouncing on its prey. It reminded him of the looks Preacher Wilson would give you when you misbehaved in church. And it worked just the same, too.

CHAPTER THREE

The Big Escape

As Benjy sauntered up to the schoolhouse, he was
hanging on to his lunch sack for dear life, because it
was the only familiar thing he had. Then he saw a
sight which settled him some. It was a real marble
game. There was a whole bunch of boys around a
circle with more marbles in it than he had ever seen
before. He was just before walking a little closer to
investigate the game when Mr. Keeper started ringing
a bell. All the kids stopped their playing and started
walking toward the door of the schoolhouse. Benjy
looked to see if any of the boys were going to leave
their marbles, but they looked like dogs after a mole,
scratching them up. It was a sight to see, and Benjy
laughed for the first time that day.

Mr. Keeper called, "First graders, line up over here behind your teacher, Mrs. Grider." She was the biggest woman Benjy had ever laid eyes on. She wasn't fat-big like some of the women in his church; she was big-big. She had gray hair that was pulled smooth and tight to the back in a ball-like shape, and she had a smile on her face that went from ear to ear. And it wasn't any short distance between those ears, either. Her arms were folded in front, and they were as big as fence posts. Benjy couldn't help but imagine her chopping wood. She could probably split a piece of oak in one blow with no trouble at all. As he watched, still from a distance, he sized her up against Mr. Keeper. She stood just as tall and big around as he was. Benjy then wondered if being big was a requirement for being a teacher, because to him they both looked like giants.

Mrs. Grider yelled out in a deep voice that carried like a coon hunter's call to his dogs, "Come on, boys and girls. Line up right here!" And she patted her oversized hands on her legs. For the second time that day, Benjy felt the urge to run for dear life. But before he had a chance, Mrs. Grider had singled him out. "Over here, young man," she called. "I know you're one of mine because you're too little to belong to anyone else." Benjy saw the other kids in line turn and look in his direction, and his face felt as hot as his momma's griddle. Thinking how small everyone looked compared to Mrs. Grider, he took a place at the end of the line.

This was the first time that Benjy had ever seen

himself around so many kids his own age, and now he was comparing himself to them. He was a bit smaller than the rest, but his new jeans and shirt looked about the same. He noticed that his cowlicked brown hair resembled some of the other boys' hair. The only difference was theirs looked to be a little neater cut, like maybe they had been town barbered, whereas Benjy's momma did the cutting on both him and his papa.

Some of the boys got tired of paying attention and began to turn around and do a little sizing up of their own. As the other boys looked him over, Benjy stuck both thumbs in his belt like his papa did and was almost on his tiptoes, trying to stretch and look bigger than he really was. Nobody had ever said it, but Benjy knew that he had more in common with his grandpa than just his smarts—they both were short and they both had the same blue eyes. Benjy was determined to start eating more green beans. His papa had always said that green beans would make you grow taller, spinach would make you stronger, and tomatoes would make you handsome. Those were the three things he hated eating the most, but he sure ate a lot of them before he got old enough to understand he was being tricked into it.

Benjy looked back at Mrs. Grider, who was searching around with her head stretched high on her neck. She looked like a turtle sunning on a log at midday, and Benjy glanced around to see what she was searching for. Whatever it was, she couldn't find it, and then she returned her attention to the kids lined up in front of her. She flashed that same big smile, revealing a mouthful of big, dark-stained teeth and one gold cap off to the side. She then said, "From now on, when you hear that bell I want you to line up quickly and stand straight and tall with your hands by your side. I don't want to see any shoving or pushing or kicking or hair pulling, okay?" When Mrs. Grider was quite sure that everyone understood the rules, she smiled with satisfaction and said, "Good. Now we'll march inside to our room and get to know one another."

Benjy tightened the grip on his lunch sack, which was already wet with sweat, and then he followed Mrs. Grider into the building. The whole sight looked like a mother duck with her babies, marching across a road and headed for a pond. Once inside the room, Benjy was amazed at what he saw. There were chairs with tops and green boards hanging on the walls. And above the boards were pictures of springtime and dogs and cats and butterflies. Mrs. Grider told them all to find a seat. Then she started asking questions about their mommas and daddies and where they lived and what their names were. When it was Benjy's turn and he told her his name, she was as quick as Mr. Keeper to make the connection between Benjy and his grandpa. She cocked one eye on him just like Mr. Keeper had done. It was the second time that day Benjy had become uncomfortable about being the grandson of Buck King. He didn't like the feeling, and he didn't like Mrs. Grider for making him feel that way. Whatever his grandpa had done, whether it was just envy or not, he had been right about one thing. It sure got under a lot of folks' skin.

Benjy felt lonesome and out of place, and he then remembered his plan of escape. He needed to tell Mrs. Grider about his being smart and all so he could leave. He knew it was going to take some nerve to get up and walk all the way to the front of the room, but his desire to leave gave him the courage he needed. As he got up, his legs were like homemade jam, and for a minute, he wasn't sure if he could make it all the way to the front. But he did. Mrs. Grider didn't notice him standing beside her, so he cleared his throat like his momma did when she was wanting his attention in church. Mrs. Grider slowly lifted her head and asked, "What do you want, Benjy?"

It wasn't Benjy's voice that spoke, and at first, he thought some girl was doing his talking for him. "Mrs. Grider," he squeaked, "I don't think I'll be needin' to stay here at school."

Before Benjy could do any explaining, Mrs. Grider frowned and said, "And what makes you think that, young man?"

Benjy's throat was dry and sticky and the words didn't come out easy. "Well, ma'am. I'm already smart enough and I don't need it."

Mrs. Grider put one of her big hands across her face as if she were trying to hold her grin in place, and then muttered, "Why, Benjy, where did you get an idea like that?"

Benjy swallowed real big and then told her about

23

being able to count and how he felt about reading and writing. He even told her about his hunting abilities, and how well he did his chores each day without being told to. He was feeling proud, and the longer he talked the better he felt. By the time he finished, Mrs. Grider was laughing so hard that tears were forming in her eyes. Benjy looked around to see what was so funny, but everyone was staring at her, looking just as confused as he was. Then Mrs. Grider wiped her eyes and said, "That's very amusing, Benjy. Now you go sit down. We've got a lot to learn today."

At first Benjy thought she had misunderstood him, and he needed to explain again. But before he could say another word, she again said, "Go on, sit down. There's more to be learned in school than just killing deer and doing your chores." And then she started to laugh again.

Benjy went back to his seat and sat down, and the more he thought about it, the madder he became. He realized Mrs. Grider was making fun of him. She didn't like his grandpa and she didn't like him, and he wasn't going to stay there any longer. So when Mrs. Grider got up and started to write something on the board, her back was turned and he knew what he had to do. The door was standing open just enough to let him squeeze through. He quietly got up from his seat, and as quickly as he could move, he escaped.

Once outside, he started running down the road, heading back home. He was thinking the whole time about how right he was to run away because he didn't like Mrs. Grider, and he wasn't going to learn anything from her no matter what. He stopped running after a while and felt much better once he turned around and saw that the school building was nowhere in sight. As much as he tried to convince himself that he was right, there was still a nagging feeling that he had done wrong. But feeling free took over.

His attention was soon focused on the many treasures that lay in the ditches on the sides of the road. He found a screw with the bolt still attached and quickly put it in his pocket, figuring it would come in handy when he and his papa worked on the truck. Then he spied two cans and laid them in the road and stomped his heels into the sides of them and continued walking with them firmly stuck on his feet. He was making an awful noise on the gravel as he walked, and it reminded him of Mrs. Grider walking across the room.

The sun was directly overhead, and Benjy figured there was still plenty of time to do some fishing with his grandpa. They would catch a mess of fish, and he would have some time to tell his grandpa the whole story about what had happened.

No sooner had he made up his mind than he heard a car coming down the road, and he eased over to the side to let it pass. But instead of going on by, the car stopped right beside him. Benjy peered over, and out of the corner of his eye, he saw Mr. Keeper himself. Just the sight of him caused Benjy to freeze stiff as an opossum playing dead. Benjy watched as Mr. Keeper leaned over the seat and opened the side door. His face was red and his forehead was covered with sweat and wrinkles caused by the awful frown on his face. Before Benjy could say anything, Mr. Keeper said in an angry voice, "Boy, where do you think you're going? You can't just get up and walk out of school any time you want to. Now get in this car."

Benjy was having cold chills right there in the dead heat of the day. He wanted to explain himself before he got in the car, and again he squeaked out, "I was just going to my grandpa's house to do some fishing."

The wrinkles and sweat seemed to multiply on Mr. Keeper's forehead. "Now, don't that just figure right. I guess your grandpa's to blame for all this. He probably thinks fishing is more important than school. It wouldn't surprise me none. Now you get in this car right away, or I'll take you home and let your momma get ahold of you."

It was the first time Benjy had thought about his momma, and he knew if she found out he was sure to get a whipping. Just the thought of it caused him to quickly get in the car. Mr. Keeper looked down at his feet and said, "Boy, get those cans off your feet and throw them outside." And he had it done before Mr. Keeper could finish telling him to do it. Benjy thought it best to stay quiet during the ride back to school. But even if he had wanted to talk, he wouldn't have been able to get a word in because Mr. Keeper was doing all the talking. He made sure Benjy understood the wrong he had done and the trouble he had caused, and the only thing he was allowed to say was, "Yes, sir. I understand now and I promise I won't do it again."

When they arrived at school, Mr. Keeper walked Benjy back to his room. Mrs. Grider was not smiling when she saw them enter, and Mr. Keeper called her out into the hall and sent Benjy to his seat. When she came back into the room, she didn't say anything to him, at least not in words. She also didn't turn her back on him again and kept a watchful eye at all times.

When the day was finally over, Mr. Keeper was waiting on the bus to take Benjy home. He did not look at Benjy when he got on, and the boy knew he was still mad. It was either the heat or exhaustion that caused Benjy to doze off, and when he awoke, they were passing his grandpa's place again. Benjy quickly raised up to see if he could see the old man, but he still was nowhere in sight. As he lowered himself back into the seat, he saw Mr. Keeper staring at him again in the mirror. Benjy was scared now, and it was a toe-curling kind of fear, because he knew Mr. Keeper was trying to decide whether or not to tell Benjy's momma about his running away from school. If he told her, Benjy knew he would get the whipping of his life. Surely, Mr. Keeper was going to allow him one mistake. After all, this was his first day and everything was new to him. Benjy tried to convince himself not to be afraid. He knew one thing for sure. He wasn't as smart as he claimed to be because, had he thought of the whipping first, he wouldn't have left his seat that morning.

Benjy caught sight of his momma and Ole Blue waiting for him by the side of the road. As the bus slowed down, Benjy moved to the front with his eyes fixed on the mirror in front of him. Mr. Keeper was watching his every move. No words passed between them, and Benjy jumped off the bus into his momma's arms, hoping to keep her away from Mr. Keeper. He heard the doors close behind him, and his fear was released in his momma's embrace. His momma kept hugging him, and Ole Blue was jumping on the both of them. Benjy had never been so happy as he was at that moment. He felt good and safe as all three of them crossed the road in front of the bus.

Benjy was telling his momma that school wasn't near as bad as he had expected. He would have told her anything to keep her from looking back at the bus. And just at the moment he had assured himself of success, he heard Mr. Keeper calling out his momma's name. Benjy stood there with Ole Blue whining at his side from lack of attention and watched his momma approach Mr. Keeper's window. Benjy knew what they were talking about.

His momma turned and came toward him, but Benjy wasn't looking at her. He was giving Mr. Keeper an eye-to-eye stare, just hoping that deep down inside, Mr. Keeper would know that Benjy would never forgive nor forget what he had done.

Then the bus left, leaving Benjy standing there alone. He turned and saw his momma bent over a sapling, and he knew what she was looking for. He wasn't going any closer than he had to, and he watched as she tore a good-sized branch from the small tree. She whipped it in the air, either testing it out or just practicing. Usually she cleaned a whipping stick down to the bark, but this time, Benjy noticed right off, she left some leaves on the end. As she walked up to him, she smiled and asked, "Well, did they have one of those televisions at school or not?"

It was the first time since morning that Benjy had remembered the television, and he wondered if his momma was trying to trick him. He shook his head and cautiously answered, "No, ma'am, I didn't see one."

His momma used one swift motion with the switch to knock a horsefly off the back of her leg, and Benjy jumped two feet in the air in a natural reaction. His momma laughed. "Boy, why are you so jumpy? I'm just trying to keep these horseflies from eating me alive."

Benjy knew he was safe now. He didn't know what Mr. Keeper had said to his momma, and he wasn't about to ask and find out. This was one of those times to leave things alone. With a sigh of relief and a shrug of his shoulders, he said, "I guess I'm still getting use to all this schooling, Momma. That's all."

CHAPTER FOUR

The Only Name Fitting for a King

Benjy came to a new understanding and appreciation for Mr. Keeper after he was spared the whipping for running away from school. He wasn't to cause Mrs. Grider or Mr. Keeper any more trouble. There was only one other incident that year, and it had to do with his name, Benjamin Bartholomew King. Benjy was quite sure that when he was born his momma put him up against a measuring stick and gave him a name as long as he was.

When Mrs. Grider became obsessed with his being able to write and spell his complete name from beginning to end, Benjy tried to explain that there wasn't any need of it. He had always been called Benjy. But Mrs. Grider insisted that even though he didn't use his real name, it was only right that he learn how to write it. She preached that it was his Christian name, and when and if he ever got to the pearly gates, he was going to have to tell God how to spell it. She said that "if" part as though she had her doubts, but Benjy knew differently. He knew that if God was smart enough to create the world and decide who was and wasn't going to get into heaven, then surely He knew such a small thing like how to spell a name.

Of course, Mrs. Grider was using God and heaven as a trick to get Benjy to agree to the task. She wasn't going to give up, so Benjy gave in. That night he began practicing, and after two pages of repeated attempts, he became frustrated. He finally asked, "Momma, what in the world were you thinking about when you tagged me with such a long name?"

His momma was busy cleaning up after supper, and amid the clatter of dishes she answered, "When you were born, I knew that you were something special and in need of a special name." She dried her hands on a dingy and ragged dish towel, and then laid it over the dishes in the draining board. Benjy watched as she untied her apron and came over to him and put her hands on his shoulders. He could tell that something was bothering her as she gave his shoulders a soft squeeze and then bent over and whispered in his ear, "It was the only name fittin' for a King." Benjy looked up at his momma and saw tears forming in her eyes. He did not know the cause of her tears, but he knew that his name had special meaning.

Pride filled him, and he became determined to

write his name better than anyone else in his class. Two pages later, he finally did it. He showed it to his momma and she agreed that it was perfect. But Benjy was not satisfied. He asked his momma to write the words, "only name fitting for a King," on another sheet of paper. Then he printed those exact words beneath his name. Once again he showed his work to his momma and proudly exclaimed, "Now it's really perfect, Momma."

Benjy ran out on the front porch and showed his writing to his papa. After a long silence, the boy finally asked, "Well, Papa, what do you think?"

The evening sun was going down, but even in the early darkness, Benjy could see the expression on his papa's face as it changed. "That's mighty good, boy, mighty good." And then he handed the paper back to Benjy and walked out into the night.

The look on Mrs. Grider's face the next morning when she saw Benjy's work told him he had finally won her approval. It was like a saving day in church as she patted his back and praised him loudly. She even passed it around the room for all the other kids to see. Benjy was as proud as an American flag blowing in the wind. But just as he was about to pop a button from all his swelling, Mrs. Grider began to take credit for his work. She said, "Benjamin Bartholomew King, I knew I could get you to do such fine work if I tried hard enough."

Benjy knew better than to argue or be disrespectful, but he wanted Mrs. Grider to know the truth. "It wasn't you who got me to do such good work,

Mrs. Grider. It was my momma." And then Benjy told her what his momma had said. Mrs. Grider took a deep breath like it was the last one she was going to get, and said, "You do have a special name, Benjy, and I just hope you learn to live up to it."

On the next Saturday, Benjy took his paper over to his grandpa's house and showed it to him. He was still full of pride and said anxiously, "Grandpa, I got me a name to be proud of and I can write it pretty good, can't I?"

Grandpa took the paper from the boy's hand and held it out a long way from his face and squinted his eyes to read it. Benjy noticed a sudden change in his grandpa as his hands started shaking and his eyes became sad. It was like he was remembering something he had just as soon forget. The look was the same one Benjy had seen on his papa's face. When his grandpa finally spoke, the words were the same, too. "That's mighty good, boy, mighty good."

Benjy was confused because his momma, papa, and grandpa had all reacted in the same way about his name. They praised his work with such sadness in their voices. "Are you all right, Grandpa?" he asked.

His grandpa nodded his head and looked away. It hurt Benjy to see him like that, but it hurt worse not knowing how to fix it. He wanted to ask questions, but he didn't want to upset his grandpa anymore. But Benjy could not stop questioning himself on the inside, over and over again that day. And the answer was always the same—nothing.

CHAPTER FIVE

Flying Is for the Birds

Mrs. Grider gave Benjy that ear-to-ear smile on the first day she saw him, and he didn't see it again until the day summer vacation was to begin. But she wasn't the only one happy about school being over. Benjy had been making plans of all the things he was going to do that summer, and his greatest ambition was to learn how to fly.

He didn't tell a soul about it, not even the kids at school. He was afraid they would try it, too, and he wanted to be the first boy ever to do it. He knew he would be famous for life and that's what held his fascination. Of course, Ole Blue knew about it. They had discussed it many times. This wasn't just any ordinary boyhood obsession. It was more like a necessity, or at least that's the way it felt to Benjy at the time. He knew that with just the right set of wings, he could do it. He searched for the perfect place to make his attempt and found it out back of his house in an old oak tree that was also his fort against attacking Indians.

For days he sat in the tree, and instead of being worried about the distance to the ground, he daydreamed about his flight. He was concerned that, once in flight, he might not have enough room to get around without hitting another tree. He knew that with all the flapping he was going to have to do, his arms would get tired. But he figured he had hauled enough wood to make him strong enough to at least get him to his grandpa's house. This was his favorite part of the daydream. He could just see the look on his grandpa's face when he saw Benjy flying down out of the sky. He would be as proud as a rooster in a full henhouse.

Benjy spent his first day of summer making his wings. He found two skinny boards and an old leather harness and went to work. He fixed two leather straps on each of the boards to make sure that his wings would not come loose during the flight. He even gathered some feathers from the chicken yard and made some flour glue to stick them on with. Once he was finished, he set the wings against the barn wall and admired his work. They were a pretty set of wings, made perfectly for flying.

That afternoon he put the wings on and went running through the barn, flapping them as hard as he could. He stirred up so much dust that he almost passed out from coughing. Ole Blue started barking wildly and running in circles around him. He got too close to Benjy's flapping, and one of the wings hit him on the head, which sent him yelping in pain and Benjy head first to the ground. He couldn't stop his fall because of the wings, and when he hit the ground, his eyes, his nose, mouth, and ears were filled with as much dirt as they could hold. It took him quite a while to get it all cleaned out, too. Ole Blue just kept barking and growling at the wings sprawled out on the ground. It wasn't long before he would just tuck his tail and run for cover every time Benjy got his wings out to practice.

Benjy's next attempts were from the top of a stall in the barn. He wasn't successful, but he wasn't discouraged because he knew it was just a matter of height. So he finally decided to make the big jump and bundled up the wings and tied them to his back. As he made the climb up the tree, Ole Blue cautiously came out of hiding and sat on his haunches below the tree and watched. He started whining, and when Benjy looked down at him, he got his first fear of flying. It wasn't because he hadn't been that high before, but because he had never been that high with the intention of jumping all the way down. It was the first time he had thought about the possibility of failure, and the more thinking he did, the more afraid he became. His papa had once told him that anything was possible if you had enough courage to try it. If you told yourself over and over, I think I can, I think I can, then it would happen.

So Benjy attached the wings to his arms, and like an opossum crawled out to the starting position. By the time he got there, he had worked up a nervous sweat, and it was running into his eyes, causing them to sting. He couldn't see, and he couldn't wipe his eyes because of his wings. He seated himself on the branch, figuring he would just fall forward when he was ready. He blinked several times until his eyes were clear again, and then started repeating over and over, "I think I can. I think I can. I think I can."

But it was not Benjy's decision to go when he did. When he started flapping, it threw him off balance, and he was gone. He only managed two good flaps before he hit the ground with a thud that rang his bell from head to toe. There was no breath left in him. Even if there had been, it wouldn't have done him any good because he couldn't move. When he finally opened his eyes, he thought he was back at school on the merry-go-round. Everything was spinning fast and he was dizzy. The only thing he could feel was Ole Blue's tongue licking his face, and along with the ringing, he heard Blue's whine. Benjy wasn't sure how long he lay there, but he wasn't in any hurry to get up.

After a while, he pulled his knees up and under him and raised himself up a little. Both of the wings had snapped in two, and feathers were scattered everywhere. The broken wings were still attached, and Benjy could not get them off fast enough. The place where the leather straps were tied to his arms was stinging like a mad bee, and the fall had tightened the knots so he couldn't untie them with his hands. He managed to get his pocket knife out and finally cut himself free. It wasn't until he tried to walk that the pain returned, and he wasn't sure if he would ever be able to walk straight again. He gathered up the wings and slowly limped back to the barn with one very important thought in his mind. Flying was for the birds. He would just have to get famous some other way.

Seeing how his attempt had been a failure, there was no need to tell anybody about it. But his papa found out anyway. Later that evening when they were doing the chores, his papa asked him why he was limping and moving so slowly. Benjy told him a half lie about jumping from a tree to escape an Indian attack. But once his papa saw the broken wings that were lying beneath the hay he was feeding to the cows, he made the connection with no problem at all. He just grinned and said, "Next time try running from those Indians."

CHAPTER SIX

The Legend of Big Sam

Benjy told his grandpa about his experience with flying, and that was the wrong thing to do. The old man nearly broke a rib trying to hold his laughter back. His face turned red and his eyes filled with tears, and when Benjy finally told him about losing his balance and falling before he intended to—well, that was all his grandpa could take. He apologized several times for laughing at Benjy, and just as soon as he would say he was sorry, he would start up again. When he finally got control of himself, he wiped his eyes and said, "Don't be ashamed of your failures, boy. You gotta have dreams and ambitions, and you gotta have enough courage to try and make them come true."

Benjy knew what his grandpa was saying, but it didn't apply to flying. He looked at his grandpa and replied, "I don't think it's courage I'm lacking in, Grandpa. After I hit that ground so hard, I thought it was more like good sense I was needing."

Those words sent his grandpa into another fit of laughter, as he shook his head in agreement. "There's some truth in those words too, boy." Then he raised his eyebrows and smiled a silly grin and added, "But if a challenge is what you're looking for—well, I've got one for you."

Benjy was more than interested in what his grandpa had in mind, but he was also a little cautious. His grandpa liked to play tricks on him, and he was good at it, too. Benjy asked, "What is it, Grandpa?"

The old man stood up and answered, "Let's go fishing and I'll tell you all about it." Benjy licked his lips in anticipation. If his next great challenge had anything to do with fishing, Benjy was ready.

Once they were out on the pond, his grandpa said, "See that stump over there with the log wedged against it?" Benjy looked to where his grandpa was pointing and nodded his head. His grandpa continued, "Well, there's a huge bass that lives there, named Big Sam. He's the biggest fish in this pond, and he's sorta like a legend, because even though everybody knows he's there, he ain't never been caught."

Benjy looked at his grandpa. When it came to fishing, he could stretch a tale like warm taffy and enjoy it just the same. Benjy was still being cautious as he asked, "How come you know Sam's there if you ain't never seen him?"

His grandpa leaned over the edge of the boat and let out a long spit of tobacco juice, which increased the brown stains already collected in the wrinkles around his mouth. He then said, "Oh, he's been hung plenty of times. He's broken more lines of mine than I like to admit to. But nobody has had the honor of eating him. He's a sly one, that's for sure."

Benjy didn't need any more convincing. If he couldn't get famous by being the first one to fly, then being the first one to catch this legend would be his claim to fame. He fished for Big Sam by day and dreamed about him at night. But after a week's worth of nothing-but-empty attempts, he was beginning to doubt that the fish even existed. However, instead of questioning his grandpa, who could get pretty angry when you doubted his stories (even when they weren't true), Benjy went to his papa. And sure enough, his papa told the story about Big Sam, much the same as his grandpa had.

That very night, Benjy dreamed that he caught Big Sam, and the next morning, his desire to make it come true was like a new-built fire in a potbellied stove. As he did his chores that morning, he was sure that it would happen that day.

Finally his momma ran out of things for him to do, and before she could think of anything else, Benjy was off in a dead run down the road. Ole Blue was running beside him, and every once in a while, they would have to stop because Ole Blue would spy a mudhole and lie belly down in it while he lapped himself up a drink of water. His hind legs stretched out in the back and his front legs did the same, as he cooled everything he owned. It looked inviting, and if it hadn't been for that fish waiting on him, Benjy would have jumped in, too.

Benjy saw his grandpa sitting in his rocker on the front porch, and he was rocking up a storm, like he was just as excited as Benjy was. As Benjy approached the porch, he proudly jumped it in one hop. And then, with what little breath was left in him, he proclaimed, "Grandpa, today's the day me and Big Sam are going to meet eyeball to eyeball."

The old man chuckled and said, "Benjy, my boy, I was figuring on the same thing, so it must be true." He then reached down beside him and picked up a new rod and reel. It was shinier than a sack of store-bought nails and even had a hook and bobber already attached to it. Benjy was speechless. The old man was grinning as he said, "Boy, if you can't catch that old fish on this new rod and reel, well, it just ain't meant to be."

Benjy was prouder than a momma cat with new-borns. He never got anything new unless it was a necessity. He took the handle of the rod that his grandpa held out to him and said, "Grandpa, you're as right as religion. This is the best rod and reel I've ever seen. I'm sure to catch Big Sam now." Benjy then hugged his grandpa long and hard and didn't even mind the bristly old whiskers that were poking his neck. The old man put his arms around the boy's waist and hugged him once and then sent his long skinny fingers up and down his ribs. The more Benjy laughed, the more his grandpa tickled him until they both almost tipped over in the rocker.

Finally his grandpa turned him loose, and then yelled out toward the pond, "Get ready, Big Sam. You're gonna meet your match today." Benjy was half crazy with excitement, and he grabbed his new rod and reel with one hand and his grandpa with the other. Benjy wanted to run and his grandpa didn't, so it was a struggle all the way to the pond.

When they reached the boat, Benjy jumped in and waited impatiently as the old man took his time, being very careful, as usual. Ole Blue started his whining like he always did, because he knew he couldn't go. Grandpa never allowed it. He said dogs were for hunting, not fishing. Benjy had only complained once, explaining that Ole Blue wasn't just a hunting dog and they were used to doing things together. But his grandpa said that two in a boat was a pleasure and three was a crowd. Benjy didn't like to leave Ole Blue, and it pained him to see his sad eyes and hear his pitiful whining. But he knew better than to ask a second time, because his grandpa would never change his mind.

Benjy paddled out to the spot they had been fishing from all week. His grandpa made a motion and whispered. "Boy, ease on around to the other side. I got a feeling Big Sam is still cooling in that shade this morning." Benjy didn't argue with the expert, even though the casting would be very hard because of the trees that hung over from the bank. His grandpa had shown him how to paddle without lifting the oar from the water. And as they approached the spot, they were as quiet as a silent prayer for salvation and just as determined. Benjy picked up his new rod and reel and baited it with a buckshot worm that was squirming worse than he was. He then looked at his grandpa for instructions, and the old man whispered, "Ain't you forgetting something?" Benjy thought for a second and then rolled his tongue around in his mouth and worked up a good spit. It landed on the worm, and his grandpa smiled with approval. He had told Benjy a long time ago that a bait was only as good as the man who spat on it, and that it was for good luck, too. Benjy was glad his grandpa had reminded him, because he was needing some luck right then.

His grandpa made a swinging side-arm motion, like he was the one doing the casting. He whispered again, "Bring that pole back to the side and then let her fly." Benjy curled his tongue out of the side of his mouth and then did as his grandpa had shown him. That glob of worm went sailing through the air, landing far away from his intentions. Even though it was his first time to try side-arm casting, he was disappointed in his attempt. He frowned at his grandpa, but the old man just put his fingers to his lips and then nodded. "That's fine, boy. Let it lay there a minute. Big Sam needs to get a whiff of that worm first. Right now, he's probably thinking it ain't worth the trouble, but you lay it in there a little closer the next time, and I guarantee, he'll be ready to bite." That made good sense to Benjy because he was that way about his momma's apple pie. She would be cooking the pie early in the morning, and just the smell of it would send his stomach into a thundering growl. Once it was set before him after supper, he would jump on it like a dog on a ham bone.

Finally his grandpa motioned for Benjy to reel it in and try once more. But his next attempt was even worse. It hit so close to Big Sam's stump that the bobber landed square in the middle of it, leaving the worm dangling down the side. Once again, his grandpa motioned for him to leave it there. "Now," he said, "that's perfect. Just let Big Sam take a good long look at it." Benjy had his doubts this time. He had never fished for anything with his bait hanging out of the water. It just wasn't natural. There wasn't anything to watch when your bobber was sitting on a stump. Benjy turned to protest when all of a sudden, the water broke wide open. When he looked back, he saw the biggest fish he had ever seen flying through the air. It grabbed that worm off the side of the stump and went back down, breaking the water with equal force. It all happened so fast and scared Benjy so much that he dropped his pole in the bottom of the boat. He went down on his knees trying to fetch it back, but it was bouncing around like popcorn in a hot skillet. The old man was hooting and hollering at the top of his lungs, and Benjy was jumping around in the boat chasing his pole and yelling, "Help me, Grandpa, help me!"

But his grandpa just laid back and roared, "It's your fish, boy, you catch him!"

Benjy caught his pole just before it went over the edge, and Big Sam gave a jerk that nearly pulled Benjy out into the water. He caught himself on the side of the boat and began to reel like crazy. His pole was bent double and every crank he made, Big Sam pulled out. Benjy dug the handle deep into his stomach and just held on for all he was worth. His grandpa was slapping his knees and hollering, "Get him, Benjy. Don't give him any slack. Get him, boy!" Benjy tried to reel once more, but it wasn't any use. So he laid back and yanked with all his might. Big Sam was more of a pro at this than Benjy was, and at the same time that Benjy was laid back and pulling as hard as he could, Big Sam turned loose of the hook. Benjy went sailing against the other side of the boat and landed flat on his rear. He looked up in time to see Big Sam come up out of the water and flip his tail as if to say, "Better luck next time."

Benjy was in the bottom of the boat close to tears. He was hurting all over, but it was his pride that hurt the most. His grandpa leaned over with his elbows propped on his knees, and with a smile on his face said, "Don't let it get the best of you, boy. You ain't

46

the first one to lose Big Sam and you won't be the last." His words did not help Benjy's feelings in the least little bit. He just lay there with his head propped up against the side of the boat and relived the whole ordeal, from Big Sam's amazing stump jump to the final flip of his tail. His grandpa sensed his disappointment and reached over and gave his head a good rubbing and once again tried to console him. "Boy, don't take it so hard. You've been had by the smartest and biggest fish in the state of Arkansas. There ain't but a handful of folks that can even lay claim to hooking Big Sam."

Benjy then realized that hooking Big Sam was as close as he was going to get to being famous, and there wasn't any use in lying there in the bottom of the boat sulking. So he slowly mustered up what strength was left in him (which wasn't much) and took his seat. He reeled his line back in and saw that the hook was as straight as his papa's aim on a buck deer. Benjy took his knife out of his pocket and cut the hook from the line and ran it through his shirt. A straight hook and a broken set of wings were all that was left of his two major adventures of the summer.

Still, even though Big Sam had gotten the best of him, the thrill and excitement of the moment was almost as strong as his disappointment. "Grandpa," he asked, "I ain't never seen a fish as big as that one. I wonder how big he really is?"

Benjy watched as his grandpa brought out his Prince Albert can and rolling papers and started to fix himself a smoke. He tapped that can, spilling out just the right amount of tobacco without dropping a speck. Then he rolled it up and licked the edge, forming a perfect cigarette, as usual. Benjy had seen this done a zillion times, but it still fascinated him somewhat. Benjy's grandpa then took a kitchen match from his shirt pocket and in one cat's swipe against the boat, the match fired up. The old man cupped his hands around the flame and sucked in his cheeks and then, like a coal-fed engine on a long train, the smoke poured out the side of his mouth. Benjy had forgotten his question, but his grandpa was pondering the answer the whole time. "Benjy, I guess that's the first time I've seen Big Sam in a while, and I'm betting he's close to twelve pounds if he's one."

That was ten fingers and a thumb and a pointer. Benjy just shook his head in disbelief as he looked out at the stump that was now as calm as an empty church. There wasn't any use trying to catch him again because he wouldn't bite twice. Besides, Benjy wanted to believe that Big Sam was just as tired as he was, because that made them both even. His grandpa was thinking the same thing as he flipped his cigarette butt in the water and said, "Come on, boy. I think you and me and Big Sam have had enough for one day."

Benjy knew his grandpa was right, and he started paddling them back to the bank. Maybe it was the excitement of the trip that caused his grandpa not to think about what he was doing. He usually stayed seated until the boat was stopped, but this time Benjy watched as he stood up on the front bench. And as they neared the bank, he grabbed a willow sapling and stuck one leg out on the bank. It was the force of that one leg hitting the ground that caused the boat to back up. Benjy watched as his grandpa's overalls tightened against his rear end as the young willow gave way to his weight, flipping him over and leaving him sprawled out between boat and bank. He was hanging there like a coon's hide that was stretched and nailed to a board for drying purposes. The only difference was, this coon was alive and spitting out cuss words with every inch he dropped. It was the funniest sight Benjy had ever seen, but he was afraid to laugh out loud. His grandpa yelled in anger, "Boy, don't just sit there. Paddle me up to the bank!" Benjy tried as hard as he could, but it wasn't any use. Every time he got his grandpa close, the willow would bend more. His grandpa was like a yo-yo. And each time he went down, his bottom got closer and closer to the water. When the old man's rear end finally touched the water, Benjy couldn't hold his laughter inside anymore. It left him helpless to paddle. His grandpa let out a whoop each time his rear touched the water and a cuss word each time he came up. Some of the words were aimed right at Benjy, but it didn't matter. Even though he realized his grandpa was going to get him good, he just lay back in the boat and had himself a good laugh. The way he fig-ured it, he owed his grandpa this one for the way he had carried on when Benjy had told him about his flying.

Benjy wasn't sure what happened next. Either the willow broke, or his grandpa let go and fell into the water. Benjy grabbed himself because he knew he was going to wet his pants, laughing so hard. His grandpa just sat there in a foot or so of water, giving Benjy a look of murder. Then it was either the sight of the boy holding himself and rocking back and forth in laughter or the thought of himself sitting in the water that brought out a belly laugh of his own that rung across the pond. Ole Blue had been dancing around, barking and whining through the whole ordeal. He was now in the water, licking the old man on the face. Benjy's grandpa finally got up and looked down at his overalls, which were glued to him like a piglet on the first tit. He then raised his arm, removed his hat, and wiped Ole Blue's slobber from his face with his shirt sleeve. As Benjy stood up, his grandpa saw that his pants were wet between his legs. He once again laughed, "Boy, what did you do, wet on yourself?"

Benjy looked down and replied, "I just couldn't help it, Grandpa. Every time I saw your hind end touch the water, I just couldn't help but laugh, and it just seeped out."

His grandpa shook his head and said, "I guess it was a sight to see me hanging on that sapling and fighting to stay dry."

Benjy's first mistake was laughing at his grandpa.

His second mistake came as he climbed toward the front of the boat and took his grandpa's outstretched hand. Just as he grabbed that hand, the old man slung him out of the boat like a rock in a full-cocked slingshot. Benjy went sailing out across the pond, yelling at the top of his lungs. When he came up, gasping and flouncing around, his grandpa was standing there, shaking his finger at him. "Next time I tell you to paddle, boy, you best be resembling a steamboat going up river in high gear!"

Benjy told the story to his momma and papa that night at supper, and his papa sure enjoyed it. He especially liked the part about the old man falling in the water. Even his momma was laughing. Benjy couldn't help but wonder if his papa and grandpa had ever had any fishing trips like this one, or had they always disliked one another so strongly. Curiosity got the best of him, and he asked, "Papa, did you and grandpa ever fish together when you were a boy?"

The grin on his papa's face disappeared. He didn't look away like he was sad or ashamed about what he had to say. "If we did go fishing together, it must have been a good time, and I don't remember too many of those." And then he got up and left the room.

CHAPTER SEVEN

Mrs. Jones

There were two important things that Benjy learned
in his first three years of schooling. He did not like
it and it did not like him. Nothing came easily for
Benjy, and because of this, nothing was fun. As he
entered the fourth grade, he was hoping for a change.

On first appearances, there didn't seem to be much
difference between Benjy's new teacher, Mrs. Jones,
and his first teacher, Mrs. Grider. They were both
big and they both did a lot of first-day smiling. Benjy
was hoping that was all they had in common. He knew
that if they were friends, Mrs. Jones already knew
plenty about him. But his fears were put to rest when
Mrs. Jones smiled at him and said, "Young man, you
look like a good leader. Would you please stand at

the front of our line and show the other students how to march inside and act nice?" Benjy knew right then and there that he and Mrs. Jones were going to get along just fine.

As they headed into the school building, Benjy was feeling better than a full-bellied pup. He looked around to see if Mrs. Grider was watching. He wanted her to see how good he was doing, but she was nowhere in sight. Once they entered the classroom, Mrs. Jones told them all to find a seat, and then she started asking the same questions about names and families that every teacher asked every year. Benjy felt his usual nervous reaction. He didn't want to tell her his full name for fear she would say something about his grandpa. He just didn't want to stir up any trouble. So when Mrs. Jones asked him his name, he just said, "Benjy."

A jeering voice from the back of the room said, "Why don't you tell her your last name?" Benjy knew it was B.J. Williams, trying to get something started.

Mrs. Jones gave a look of warning to B.J. and then asked, "Well, Benjy, do you have a last name?"

Now it was Benjy's turn to pause. Finally he said, "Yes, ma'am, my last name is King."

Benjy looked away and waited for Mrs. Jones to make the connection and say something about his grandpa. But she didn't. Instead she said, "Well, that's a good name, Benjy King."

Mrs. Jones had passed the true test and Benjy smiled back at her and said, "Thank you, ma'am. I like your name, too." Mrs. Jones laughed and some of the other kids giggled along with her. Even though he didn't know what they were laughing about, Benjy joined in. It was like heaven and Mrs. Jones was an angel.

Mrs. Jones was a good teacher and Benjy liked her, but it didn't make learning any easier for him. He tried very hard to please her, but learning to read new words was the hardest thing he had ever done. Mrs. Jones had flash cards with words on them that she would hold up before the class. Benjy did fine if the whole class was answering, but when he had to answer by himself, he couldn't make the words come out right. He tried to memorize the words in order, but then Mrs. Jones would mix up the cards and he would get as flustered as a beaver in a dry creek.

Mrs. Jones had the patience of a momma cat, and every spare minute of the day, she worked with Benjy. With every sign of improvement, she praised him with gold stars and let him do extra things in the class. By the end of the year, Benjy could read the words on the cards. He still wasn't very good at it, but given the time and a little help in getting started, he could do it.

On the last day of school, Benjy was happy about getting out for summer vacation, but sad to be leaving Mrs. Jones. That morning he asked his momma if he could have a jar of blackberry jam to give to Mrs. Jones and his momma gave him two. She said, "You tell Mrs. Jones the other one is from me for all the extra help she's given you."

Benjy waited until the end of the day and then gave the jars of jam to Mrs. Jones. You would have thought they were diamonds. She gave Benjy a big hug and squeezed him up tighter than a knot. She then said, "I'm going to miss you, Benjy King. You're a fine boy. I don't care what anybody else says about you or your grandpa. You're a fine boy." Benjy turned and waved good-bye more than once as he left the school building. He now knew that Mrs. Jones had known about him all along from Mrs. Grider and Mr. Keeper. And she knew about his grandpa too, and it didn't make any difference to her.

As Benjy walked out into the school yard, he was feeling good. Not just good because the school year was over, but good because he had liked it so much. Instead of going to the bus, Benjy decided to spend some time on the playground. Even though shooting marbles was by far his best subject in school, he had stopped playing with the boys at school a long time ago. It was a part of his attempt to remain invisible. The less attention he drew to himself, the better he liked it. But today was different as Benjy watched B.J. Williams throw his best aggie shooter into the ring. It was the prize marble that Benjy and everyone else in school had secretly yearned to own for years. But B.J. was a bully and had never given anyone the chance to win it.

Benjy knew he could win, so he joined in the game,

much to the surprise of everyone standing around. And that was when the trouble began. It was too late for B.J. to retrieve his shooter without being called a chicken, which would have been instant death to his fearless reputation. No one messed with B.J. and he had a passel of boys who followed him around like nursing pups. They didn't do it out of respect. It was more out of fear. It was better to be one of B.J.'s sidekicks than one of his victims. Benjy had chosen to be neither until this day.

As the game began, it was obvious that all four boys playing were shooting for the same marble. The circle was drawn larger than usual, and the first boy to knock the aggie shooter out of the circle would win. On Benjy's second try, he succeeded, but just as he reached over to pick up the prized marble, B.J. snatched it up and put it in his pocket. Benjy was quick to his feet, not really knowing what he was going to do. He was nervous as he realized that now the real game was about to begin, and it was one he could not win. Benjy tried to remain calm as he spoke. "Give me my marble, B.J. I won it fair and square."

B.J. smiled with pleasure. Fighting was his best subject in school. "It ain't your marble because you cheated. Your knuckles were over the line when you shot and hit it. The game's over and you lost." B.J. kicked all the remaining marbles in the circle and they scattered everywhere. This was his show of power, so that no one would dispute his word. And it worked. The boys standing around slowly moved behind B.J. Even though Benjy was mad for being called a cheater, he was not going to get into a fight over a marble, and he turned and walked away. It was time to become invisible again.

It would have been over except that B.J., realizing he had won too easily, was not about to let it die. In his usual loud and obnoxious voice, B.J. jeered, "That's it. Walk away. You're a cheater and a loser, just like your grandpa. He's a no-count—everybody in this town knows it. And you're just like him."

Benjy had his back to B.J. when those words lit him up like a match to gasoline. At that one moment every bad thing that had ever been said about his grandpa, every evil look he had seen at just the mention of Grandpa's name, and every time he had been shunned for being the grandson of Buck King, exploded inside Benjy. This was the first time any kid had dared to say something about his grandpa directly to him. Benjy's thinking was mixed-up as he slowly turned and said, "You take every word back that you just said, B.J., or I'll . . ."

But before Benjy could finish, B.J., the master of control and power, said, "Or you'll what? What are you going to do? You ain't man enough to fight me. Like I said, you're just like that old man you call your grandpa. My daddy says he's a good-for-nothing, and I say you're just like him."

Mr. Keeper was honking the horn on the bus, and Benjy knew he had to leave or he would miss it. But he took the challenge B.J. had made. It was a matter of pride and honor and standing up for someone you loved, and Benjy knew it was the right thing to do. "I'll fight you, B.J. I've got to catch the bus right now, but you name the time and the place and I'll fight you."

B.J. smiled with pleasure. "Well, how about tomorrow? Meet me at the Pine Grove at Jackson's Curve. I'll be there at ten o'clock and if you don't chicken out before then, we'll say the winner gets the marble." B.J. was proud of himself for adding the marble as the prize. He knew Benjy had not cheated, and this way he could win back his marble fair and square, without any guilt. Tomorrow was the first day of summer vacation. It was perfect.

CHAPTER EIGHT

Ready or Not

Benjy awoke the next morning with the same thought he had gone to bed with. Today he was going to fight his first fight. He felt nothing but dread and fear as his toes began to curl. He knew he was going to get beat up, and if he had thought of that at the time of the challenge, he probably would have backed down (or better yet, kept his mouth shut). But now that was impossible.

The smell of bacon and biscuits drifted through his room, making him realize how really afraid he was. His appetite was gone. He heard his momma calling that breakfast was ready. If he didn't eat, she would surely send him back to bed, thinking he was coming down with some incurable disease. Or worse than that, she would know something was bothering him, and question him until he would have to lie to her. Telling her the truth would never work. She would not let him fight. But if she learned the truth behind the fight, Benjy would have more to fear than B.J. Williams.

Benjy's heart jumped when he heard his momma's voice again. She was standing at the door and said, "Boy, what's the matter with you? It's your first day of summer vacation and you're still laying in here on your bed. I figured by now you'd have them chores done and headed to the woods. Are you feeling okay? You ain't even had breakfast yet."

Benjy tried to recover as quickly as possible. The questions had already started and if he didn't put her mind at ease, he would never escape without her finding out the truth. A false smile came across his face. "There ain't nothing wrong with me. I was laying here seeing how it feels to be lazy. I got all day to do chores and roam the woods. That's what's so nice about summer vacation."

His momma took the bait and she laughed. "Boy, get up and eat your breakfast before I throw it out to Ole Blue."

Benjy didn't waste any time getting to the table. His insides were flopping like a fish out of water, and even though it wasn't easy, he choked one egg down just so his momma wouldn't get suspicious. He ate one biscuit and slipped the other one into his pocket for Ole Blue. It was the milk that got to him. It was already warm and just as it was going down, Benjy thought of what would happen if B.J. hit him in the stomach. The boy gagged and had to stop drinking. He wondered if just maybe this once his momma would let him be excused from the table without finishing his milk. But as usual, his momma was doing mind-reading tricks. She turned from the sink and said, "Son, you're going to be at the table until supper if you don't drink that milk. Waste not, want not. We ain't feeding that milk cow out there just so you can waste it."

Benjy closed his eyes and emptied the glass, with the thought that this was probably going to be the easiest thing he did all day. As he got up from the table his momma asked, "What are you going to do today besides roam the woods with Ole Blue?"

The boy was trying so hard to avoid the truth that he didn't think before he answered. "Well, I'll probably go over to Grandpa's and do some fishing." He knew better than to mention his grandpa's name, but at least it stopped his momma's questioning. She gave him a hard look and turned back to her dishes.

Benjy left the room before his momma had a chance to ask any more questions. He greeted Ole Blue and fed him his biscuit, and then started doing his chores, with Ole Blue taking every step that he took. The boy didn't want his dog to come along to the fight for fear of what Ole Blue might do, or worse, what the other boys might do to his dog. But if he left him tied up at the house his momma was sure to know something was wrong, because Benjy never left the house without Ole Blue. Benjy found some rope in the barn and put it in his pocket. He knew B.J. would not show up alone. It wouldn't be any fun for him to beat up Benjy without someone there to watch. And maybe taking Ole Blue along wasn't such a bad idea. At least Benjy would have one on his side.

CHAPTER NINE

The Fight

It was a three-mile walk to Jackson's Curve, and for Benjy, that meant too much time for thinking. He wished that he had gone ahead and fought B.J. the day it happened. He was mad then, and out of anger he might have been able to land a couple of punches. But now his anger was gone. He knew that B.J.'s remarks about his grandpa were just a repeat of what he had heard from his own father. And it wasn't anything that Benjy hadn't heard before. No one really knew his grandpa like Benjy, and until they did, they would continue to think the worst of him.

Thinking of this now made fighting senseless. It wasn't Benjy's nature to fight or to hurt anybody. He had never even hit his dog. And even though he killed animals for food, there was never a time that he didn't feel a twinge of pain when he saw a dead animal. And that's why he never hunted for pleasure. When his momma told him they needed a rabbit or a squirrel, he only killed what was necessary for a meal. Benjy's papa had taught him at an early age the laws of nature. One of them was never to take from Mother Nature more than you needed, and she would always provide for you.

Benjy tried hard to think of a reason why he should go on. He did not want to start the next school year being known as a chicken for not showing up, because he knew that B.J. and his gang would be unmerciful with their jeers. They would not let it die, and being labeled a chicken would stick with him forever. He was already the "dumb kid" and he didn't need another label to live with.

As Benjy rounded Jackson's Curve, the sight was just as he suspected. A group of boys stood circled in the Pine Grove, with B.J. in the middle. Some were older and all were bigger than Benjy. At that moment, they seemed like giants. At first they didn't notice Benjy watching as they threw their pocket-knives at one of the trees. B.J. could be heard above the rest. He bragged when his knife hit and stuck squarely in the tree, "That's three in a row, boys, pay up." As Benjy watched the boys reaching in their pockets to pull out money to give to B.J., he wondered if B.J. ever lost at anything.

The bully proudly stuffed the money in his own pocket, then he turned and saw Benjy standing across the road. Benjy's heart began to race. B.J., anxious to establish himself as the fearless and dominating opponent, quickly called out, "Well, looky here, fellows. Benjy ain't no scared chicken like we thought he was. I don't guess he's ever heard the saying, 'It's better to be a live chicken than a dead hero.' " All the boys laughed and slapped B.J. on the back. This was a sign of encouragement and all B.J. needed. He looked at Ole Blue and then jeered, "Did you bring your dog along to do your fighting for you or was you just too scared to come by yourself?" And once again the boys hooted in delight.

Never had Benjy felt so intimidated. He didn't know whether to run for his life or stay and fight. He hated B.J. for what he was saying and he hated himself worse for allowing him to say it. All he wanted now was to get it over with and go home. He reached in his pocket and pulled the rope out and tied it around Ole Blue's collar and then tied the other end to a pine tree away from all the boys. Ole Blue didn't like it and immediately started trying to free himself as Benjy walked away to face the bully. He stopped right in front of B.J. and said, "I ain't no chicken." And it was as if the words transformed him as he spoke them. Now he decided to use a few tactics of his own. "I'm here to fight you because of all the bad things you said about me and my grandpa. But if you'll take them all back, I'll leave you alone." Benjy could not believe what he was saying. Even though the fear was raging inside of him, he spoke like he was the one in control of the whole situation.

But Benjy's challenging words only riled B.J. The

bully quickly growled back through gritted teeth, "I ain't taking nothing back. I said your grandpa was a worthless no-count and I said the same thing about you. Neither one of you is worth spit." And then he spat on the ground at Benjy's feet.

All Benjy's feelings came to a head like a festered boil. He raised his arms to protect himself and doubled up his fists. He knew he would not be the first one to throw a punch. He didn't even know how. B.J. started circling Benjy as if he were waiting for just the right time and place, and Benjy moved defensively, hoping he would never find it. But B.J. was quick and experienced and his first jab caught Benjy in the chin. It was a long-reach punch and just grazed the boy's face. But it stung just the same. Benjy knew if B.J. ever hit him full force, it would break something. And it was just that thought that caused him to lunge at the bully and grab him around the shoulders.

Fortunately for Benjy, he caught B.J. off guard, and the two of them fell to the ground. Benjy had the advantage now. If there was one thing he knew how to do, it was wrestle. He and his papa had wrestled many times in the front yard, and though it was just for fun, Benjy had learned how to protect himself from letting his papa tickle him and gain the victory.

Benjy was well aware that B.J., who was now squirming beneath him, had no intentions of tickling him. The bully was pulling hair and scratching and pinching everything he could find. He was a dog after a mole, and Benjy was the mole. Benjy heard the other boys hollering with excitement, and then one of them said, "It looks like Benjy is getting the best of him." That was all B.J. needed to hear. Before Benjy knew what had happened, B.J. was on top of him and had his arms pinned to the ground. His face was red and sweating and he was swearing with each breath he took. Benjy sensed that the end was near and made one last attempt to free himself.

It was about that time that Ole Blue let out a yelp like he was hurting, and Benjy instinctively looked over, for fear one of the other boys had hurt Ole Blue. This was the chance B.J. had been looking for. He let go of Benjy's arm long enough to throw one good punch, which caught Benjy smack in the left eye. The pain was every bit as unbearable as Benjy thought it would be. He let out a long scream that could be heard for miles around. He took his free hand, and instead of trying to fight back, he covered his face and eyes. And then Benjy was free. B.J. jumped up and Benjy was left rolling on the ground in pain, with his hands covering his face.

At first the boy thought it was his scream that had scared B.J. and caused him to get up so fast, and Benjy was just about to let out another one when he heard a familiar voice. "What's going on here, boys?" Benjy looked up at his grandpa through one eye. The other was swollen shut. He was so stunned that he couldn't move or speak. He looked at B.J. and for the first time in his life, he saw real fear on the face of the bully.

His grandpa looked at the other boys and asked again, "Somebody want to tell me what this fight is all about?" No one was about to tell him that the fight was about him, least of all B.J. The bully just stood there in fear someone would speak up. The old man reached down and helped Benjy up from the ground. He pushed the hair from his grandson's face to get a better look at his eye. He directed his question straight at Benjy. "I ain't gonna ask again, boy. What are you two fighting about?"

Benjy hesitated in his answer as he looked at B.J. The bully's face was the picture of fright, but there was pleading in his eyes. B.J.'s father worked for the old man. The last thing he wanted was for Benjy to tell his grandpa the truth. Now it was Benjy who was in control of the situation. Now he could get his revenge by telling his grandpa everything B.J. had said about him, or he could win this fight by saving B.J.'s hide. He knew that if he lied, B.J. would never bother him again. He would always owe him one, and even a bully would honor that. Benjy did not look at his grandpa as he spoke, but kept his eye on B.J. to make sure the bully understood the favor he was doing him. "We're fighting because he said some things that I didn't like."

The old man said, "Well, by the looks of things, you got a black eye and he ain't got a scratch on him, so I'd say you ain't changed his way of thinking just yet. If this is the only way you know how to do that, and you think if you beat him up he's gonna change, well—I ain't gonna stand in your way. I'll just step over here and y'all go ahead with your fighting. Go on, now. I'd like to see a good fight. And when one of you finally tells the other one he was right, then the fight will be over." And then his grandpa took several steps away and stopped as if he were waiting.

Benjy felt as dumb as a comb in a bald man's pocket. His grandpa had made his point. It didn't matter who won the fight. Neither one of them was ever going to believe that the other one was right. Benjy couldn't think of anything to say, so he just walked over to the pine tree and untied Ole Blue and started to walk to his grandpa's truck.

He heard B.J. call his name, and when he turned around, a marble was flying through the air, shining and sparkling like a diamond in the sunlight. Even with one bad eye, Benjy caught it and held it in his hand. At first, he was surprised by the gesture, and then he realized this was B.J.'s way of repaying him for the favor he had just done him by not telling his grandpa the truth. He started to throw the marble back. He wanted B.J. to remain in his debt forever. But then Benjy remembered the marble game in which he had won the marble fair and square. It was his and he was going to keep it. He wanted to believe that this was the real reason B.J. had thrown the marble to him, and he looked at the bully to see if there was any hint of the real reason on his face.

But B.J. had already turned and walked away, with his gang following in his footsteps. One of the boys in the group asked, "Hey, why did you give him the marble? He didn't win the fight."

B.J. turned and snarled at him, "You want to make something of it?"

CHAPTER TEN

Double Trouble

Buck King followed Benjy to the truck. When his grandfather finally asked, "How's the eye?" Benjy just mumbled back, "It's okay."

Trying to keep the boy talking, the old man said, "Well, it doesn't look okay. You've got a real shiner. It's black and blue and swollen real bad. That other boy must have said something really terrible for you to fight with him. He was twice your size and probably older than you. I guess you knew ahead of time your chances of winning weren't too good."

The old man wasn't saying anything Benjy didn't already know, and he knew his grandpa was fishing for him to tell him the truth. But Benjy just nodded his head and remained silent. Finally the old man had

had enough and he said, "Tell me the real reason you was fighting today, boy."

Benjy stared out the window and thought a long time before answering. He knew the truth would make his grandpa mad, and maybe even hurt his feelings. But he also knew that it could open the doors, and give him a chance to find out why B.J. and everybody else felt the way they did about the old man. So he told his grandpa the real reason behind the fight. And the whole time he was doing it, he wished that he hadn't. His grandpa's face became dull and pale as if Benjy's words were sucking the life out of him. Even the blue of his eyes became misty and tired looking. Finally he said, "Benjy, I thank you for standing up for me today. I understand why you did it, but it was wrong. You'll have to get used to folks saying bad things about me, but I already told you it's just because they're envious of what I own. A poor man can never own what I own and so he just has to find other ways to bring me down. They lie about me and hope that in some way, by putting me down, it raises them up. But it only works like that when you allow it to, by getting down on their level and fighting with them. That's why fighting is wrong."

The old man stopped and looked to see if his grandson understood what he was saying, but the boy kept his head turned. He already knew that fighting was wrong and why. And that was the only truth he heard. He wanted to believe his grandpa, but something inside of him said the rest of it was just lies. The boy stopped listening and the old man stopped talking. They rode the rest of the way home in silence.

His grandpa stopped the truck on the county road and let Benjy out. Both of them knew if his grandpa drove the rest of the way to his house and his momma saw Benjy getting out of the truck with a black eye, there would be trouble. The boy felt the stiffness in his body as he climbed out and let the tailgate down for Ole Blue. As they walked around to the side of the truck, his grandpa said, "Remember, Benjy, I can take anything anybody has to say about me. I've been living with it for a long time now, and you don't have to fight for me." And as he drove away, he hollered back, "Come by later this week and we'll do some fishing." And then he gave his Stetson hat a tug and drove away.

Benjy knew that more trouble was about to begin as he approached his house. Had he not gotten the black eye, his momma and papa would never have had to know about the fight. Benjy's first thought was to lie about it. He could tell them that he and Ole Blue were playing and his dog's head had caught him in the eye. Or maybe he could say that he had run into a tree while playing in the woods. But the more Benjy thought about it, the more he hated the idea of lying. Somehow it just didn't seem right. He had always been raised to be honest, and if his parents found out later that he had lied, it would just mean double trouble. He also knew that if he lied, he would have to deal with the guilt. It just seemed better to get it all over with now by telling the truth.

His momma was on the porch peeling apples. When she saw him, she was quick to her feet and ran halfway across the yard. She was frantic as she asked, "Son, what happened to your eye? It looks terrible. Get in out of this sun and let me have a look at it." As she helped him across the yard, she asked, "Did you fall down or run into something?" She sat Benjy in the rocking chair and put her hand under his chin and raised his head. "Oh, Benjy, it's awful. Tell me what happened."

Benjy lowered his head and said, "I was in a fight this morning." He didn't have a chance to say another word.

His momma's mouth flew open in disbelief. "I know better than that. Now you tell me the truth. You didn't get into a fight. There's nobody around here for you to fight. . . ." She stopped and put her hand to her mouth in horror. "You said you were going to your grandpa's. . . . Did he do this to you? You tell me the truth, boy. I mean you tell me the truth right now!"

Benjy couldn't believe what his momma was saying. How could she think that his grandpa would hit him! He quickly answered, "*No!* My grandpa would never hurt me. How can you say something like that, Momma? That's a terrible thing to say."

His momma hesitated and became flustered. "I . . . I don't know. I mean, what else was I suppose to think?"

Benjy was upset and started to cry. "I told you I

was in a fight. Me and Billy Joe Williams had a fight today over a marble. I won it in a game and he said I cheated and started calling me names, so we fought." Benjy did not tell her the rest of the story. After what she had just said about his grandpa, he couldn't tell her the real reason.

This time his momma believed him, and her concern over his eye quickly changed to anger. There was fire in her eyes and her words were like sparks as they flew from her lips. "I raised you better than that, boy. The Good Book says to turn the other cheek, and I always told you never to fight. Fighting doesn't solve a thing. I'm ashamed of you and so disappointed. When I get finished with you, that eye ain't gonna be the only thing hurting." And she left him on the porch and went to the edge of the woods.

Benjy knew she was going to get a switch. He was going to get the whipping of his life, and he knew he had it coming. He watched as she went from tree to tree, careful in her choice of branches. She then turned and sternly called out, "Come here right now, Benjamin!" Benjy knew she meant business, because the only time she called him by his full name was when he was in deep trouble. The boy slowly got up and walked over to where she was standing. He started to protest and try to explain things to her, but then bent over and gritted his teeth, determined not to cry. His momma said, "This whipping is for lying to me this morning about where you were going and for fighting over something so silly as a marble game and name calling." Benjy closed his eyes and waited, but his momma didn't hit him. She stopped in midair and said, "Go on to the house. I'm thinking this is one whipping I'll leave up to your daddy."

CHAPTER ELEVEN

An Understanding Man

Benjy was left there with his rear end up in the air and a switch lying beside his feet. Now, most boys would have started doing rollovers from being spared that whipping, but that was not the case with Benjy. He knew that now he would have to spend the rest of the day waiting for his papa to come home. He picked up the switch and almost ran to his momma, begging for the whipping. He wanted to get it over with now. Of course, his momma knew that the waiting would be worse than any whipping she could give him, and she was just as right as a good deed in her thinking.

Benjy carried this burden on the inside for the rest of the day. He didn't like it when his momma was mad at him. She never spoke to him, and her silence was always a constant reminder that he had done wrong. It still bothered him that he hadn't told his momma the complete truth. He wondered if it was really lying when you told part of the truth and just left out some of the details. He thought about going inside and trying again, hoping by now she had calmed down some. But there was too much fear that the truth would just make things worse, if that was possible.

Benjy did his chores better than ever before, knowing full well it wasn't going to get him out of trouble. He was just needing to do something right in the middle of all the wrong he had managed in one day. The rumbling of his papa's truck coming up the road brought an equal rumbling all over him. And even though he wasn't looking forward to the whipping, he was glad that it would soon be over. Benjy decided that it might help a little if his papa saw him hard at work, so he started stacking up the wood that his papa had split on the past Saturday. It wasn't one of his everyday chores, and he figured his papa would be proud to see him doing something without being told. His papa climbed out of the truck and gave him a wave, which Benjy returned, making sure he kept his swollen eye out of sight. His papa had his black lunch pail in his hand and an old shirt thrown over his shoulder. His overalls were dirty and stained, much like his face, which just looked plain tired. In an exhausted voice he hollered out, "Hey, Benjy. I reckon this year of schooling done you some good if it taught you to do that stacking without being told."

Benjy knew right then and there that he should have called his papa over and told him about the fight, but it just wasn't in him. So instead, he just smiled weakly and said, "I guess so, Papa." His papa grinned and walked on into the house.

After a while, his momma hollered out the front door that supper was ready, and even though Benjy was as hungry as a bear out of hibernation, this was one meal he wouldn't have minded missing. He knew nothing would be said at suppertime, because his papa had a rule that family business was never mixed with pleasure, and eating was definitely his papa's pleasure. Benjy let out a deep sigh and went into the house and washed his hands.

The first thing he did after seating himself was to check his papa's face for a sign of how much trouble he was in. But there weren't any signs. His papa just looked at his eye, said the blessing, and started to pass the food. Benjy said his own blessing, but it wasn't about being thankful for the food. It was more like begging God to give his papa an understanding heart.

His papa ate like there wasn't any more food in the world and didn't say a thing. Benjy kept his head down and picked at his food. For the boy, suppertime lasted an eternity. Finally his papa took a long swallow of tea and sucked on his teeth like he was cleaning them. It always sounded like a playful squirrel without a care in the world. Benjy knew his papa was staring at him, because he felt his eyes burning through him. Benjy looked up and watched as his papa leaned his chair back on two legs and hooked his thumbs under his belt. Benjy knew then that his papa was fully prepared to whip him; he had already changed from his overalls to his jeans, for the sole purpose of wearing his leather belt. Most times Benjy would watch his papa's movements during supper, just longing for the day he would be able to make squirrel-like noises and lean his chair back. But the only thing making an impression on him that night was the belt his papa was wearing. The thud of the chair hitting the floor caused Benjy's heart to jump like a bullfrog after a bug. Then he heard his papa say, "Momma, that was a mighty fine meal." He then looked at his son and said, "Benjy, I'll be waiting outside when you get finished eating." Then he stood up, stretched his arms way out in the air, and patted his stomach and left. Benjy knew that the stretching meant his papa was getting warmed up for the whipping. One thing was for sure. Those last words spoken meant Benjy was finished eating, whether he was still hungry or not. Benjy asked his momma if he could be excused from the table and she just nodded. He knew once he had been punished, she would be speaking to him again, and he was glad to be getting it all over with.

He walked outside and saw his papa sitting on the front porch, cutting a plug of tobacco off his square. Benjy watched as he held that plug on the knife blade, raised it up to his mouth and stuck it in, bringing out a clean blade. It was amazing how he did that without cutting off his tongue. Then his papa mumbled for him to sit down, and patted the porch floor next to him. Benjy watched him as he had always done, ever since he could remember. His papa worked that plug around his mouth and then spat out a long, slimy brown streak. It hit the dusty ground and disappeared. Then his papa said, "Boy, I reckon by now you know you done wrong by fighting today."

Benjy's head was hanging low as he replied, "Yes, sir, I do."

There was a long pause and then his papa spit again. It landed dead center of the same spot he had hit before. He still was not looking at his son. Benjy looked up at his tired face and watched as he rubbed his beard. Then he looked at Benjy for the first time and said, "You want to tell me what happened and why you did it?"

Benjy finally had his chance to tell the whole truth, and this time he would do it. He told the story from start to finish, including the part about what was said about his grandpa. Benjy also explained that he had not told his momma everything, and why. His papa just sat and listened, not saying a word.

Benjy stopped talking and quietly waited for his papa's response. His papa took his time in speaking, and then calmly said, "Son, what you did today was wrong and there is no excuse for it. You might as well get used to the fact that people don't have a very high opinion of your grandpa, but you can't use it as an excuse to do wrong. You don't have to be ashamed of it, either. If you do wrong every time someone says something about your grandpa or treats you differently because of him, then you make them think that you are just like him, and you're not. You are my boy first, and I've raised you better. You make sure you live up to your own reputation, and people will soon judge you for that instead of your being the grandson of Buck King. Does that make sense to you, son?"

It was as clear as the sound of the school bell. Benjy knew what his papa was saying, because it was the same point his grandpa had made earlier. Once again, Benjy was reminded of how much the two men were alike, and again, the boy felt the same questions in his heart. Now seemed like the right time to ask. "Papa, I understand what you're saying and I promise you I won't never let it happen again." Then Benjy stopped. He was sure he wanted to ask the question, but a part of him was not sure if he wanted to know the answer. It was a hard decision, but he gave in to his yearning. "Papa . . . I know I ain't suppose to ask, but why is it people don't like Grandpa? Maybe if I knew why folks feel the way they do, I could take it a little better. It ain't easy to listen to that kind of talk and not do nothing about it."

His papa stood up and then turned to face his son. His voice was full of warning. "If you don't learn anything else today, you learn to leave well enough alone. This ain't about your grandpa. It's about you fighting today. And I aim to make sure it never happens again."

Benjy knew what his papa meant. His question would not be answered, and it was time for his whipping. He stood up and then bent over for the second time that day. He held out his arm so his papa could hold it as he always did when he whipped him. His papa took the arm and pulled the boy next to him. Benjy was not sure of what was happening. Then his papa gently put his hand under his chin and raised his face upward. His voice was like a whisper of wind through the tall pines. "I ain't gonna whip you, son. You were wrong to fight today, but I understand why you did it. I'm not saying it was right, and I hope you know not to let it ever happen again. But if it should, then I guess we both know what to expect."

Benjy nodded his head, still cupped in the gentle embrace of his papa's strong and calloused hands. He felt his papa's fingers gently rub over his swollen eye and the touch was loving and caused no pain. His eye would not heal for some time, but inside of him the pain disappeared. Tears started coming from nowhere. At first he thought the tears were happy ones from being spared a whipping, but that wasn't the reason at all. It was just knowing that his papa was an understanding man whom he could always trust. He hugged his papa long and hard, and the big man blinked away his own tears as he remembered a time long ago.

CHAPTER TWELVE

Coot Hunter: A Legend in His Own Time

There weren't many people who had the honor of calling Coot Hunter their friend, but Benjy's papa was one of the fortunate ones. Coot didn't have kinfolks in these parts and he lived back off in the woods by himself. He had some of the best hunting dogs in the county and made his living off hunting and trapping animals. But he wasn't near as famous for his hunting as he was for his storytelling. Coot didn't come out of the woods very often, and he didn't like being around people for any length of time. Many times Joe King had asked Coot to come to deer camp, but he would just cock his head and say, "Too many folks in the woods is like a bad case of chiggers and causes me to itch and scratch just the same."

The only time he would appear at the camps was on rare occasions when all the men and boys were sitting around the fire at night, telling stories and seeing who could tell the biggest lie. Ole Coot would just walk up out of nowhere and sit down and help himself to a cup of coffee. And then before you knew it, he would begin telling one of his own stories, and grown men and boys alike would sit with hanging jaws and bugging eyes. Once he finished, he would reach up and give his hat a tug to the side and thank everyone kindly for the company. Then he would walk out into the woods and disappear, leaving everyone feeling as though he had been visited by a ghost. One thing for sure, there wasn't any need for more story telling after Coot had told one or two of his own. No one was willing to try and outdo him. There just wasn't any need in it or any way it could be done.

But it wasn't just the way Ole Coot told a story that made people listen. There was something special about each story, like he wasn't just talking about hunting but about life itself. He'd tell a story about one of his dogs dying, and everyone listening would get a lump in his throat that couldn't be swallowed. And before bedding down that night, every dog in camp would get a good rubbing and a kind word or two.

Once Coot told a story about deer hunting, and somehow the story ended up being a good lesson on killing. Ole Coot said, "I don't reckon there's no one here who loves hunting better than me. But killing just for the sake of killing, well, I reckon that to be a downright sin. And when the day comes that us menfolk start killing more than we need for food or trading purposes, we'll sure enough be offending Mother Nature."

The way that Coot Hunter and Benjy met for the first time was a bit embarrassing, but Benjy would never forget it. It happened while Benjy and Ole Blue were in the barn playing chase around the bales of hay. They both heard a truck coming up the road and came sauntering out of the barn about the same time Coot was crawling out of his truck. Benjy wasn't sure whether he should run and hide or get to the house to protect his momma. His papa was gone to town and his momma was canning food. Either she didn't hear Coot coming, or she was thinking it was his papa who drove up. Coot didn't see Benjy at first, and Benjy stepped back into the barn, hoping to keep it that way. He didn't know who Coot was or what he was doing at their house, but he did know that Coot was the meanest- and ugliest-looking man he had ever laid eyes on.

Coot had one eye bigger than the other, and it sort of bulged out like it was the only one doing the looking. The other eye was just sitting there like it didn't serve any purpose. He wore his hat cocked to one side, covering that small eye and leaving plenty of room for the big one. His eyes were scary enough, but it was the long scar running down from that covered eye that made him look so mean. It went clear down to his chin, and even though he had a beard that hung halfway down his chest, there wasn't a single hair growing in that scar. That made him look even meaner. As Benjy stood observing Coot from behind the barn door, his imagination got the best of him. He figured if a man looked that bad he must be a no-count, up to no good.

Benjy watched as Coot cocked his head over to one side, so he could see better with his one big eye. He was looking the place over, and Benjy was then convinced that Coot was looking to see what he could steal. Benjy's heart was beating too fast and his knees were weak, but he knew it was his job to make sure that Coot didn't touch a thing.

Quickly Benjy began looking around the barn for something to hit Coot with, and he spied an old ax handle in the corner. It was his nervousness that caused him to turn too quickly and catch Ole Blue off guard. And the next thing Benjy knew, he and Ole Blue were tangled up in a mess. Ole Blue let out a howl, and just as Benjy was falling to the ground, he reached for the barn wall to catch himself. This sent a whole row of tools crashing down on top of him. He looked up just in time to see a big hammer headed straight for his face, and he threw up his arm to protect himself. It hit the funny bone in his elbow, and he let out a squawl twice as loud as Ole Blue's.

He was lying there, rolling back and forth with his eyes shut tight in pain when he heard a low, gruff voice say, "You all right, boy?"

Benjy's heart jumped straight out of him. He scrambled to his feet, trying to keep one eye on Coot and looking for the hammer at the same time. Coot's face was even uglier up close. As he smiled at Benjy, he revealed a mouth of teeth that were either rotted or gone. Twice, chills crawled up and down Benjy's spine. Coot said, "Boy, ain't no need to be afraid. I ain't gonna hurt you, least ways not any worser than you done to yourself already." It wasn't his words that settled Benjy's fear but the sight of Ole Blue wagging his tail and licking Coot's hand. Ole Blue's sense about people had never failed Benjy yet. And if Coot was intending to do Benjy any harm or was really a no-count, Ole Blue would have been the first to know it.

Benjy knew all this, but just looking at Coot kept him second-guessing his dog's better judgment. Benjy tried to act like he wasn't scared, but as he reached down to brush himself off, he picked up the hammer, as well as a big crowbar. Coot squatted down, not paying any attention to Benjy, and gave Ole Blue a good rub on the head. Then he said, "This here's a mighty fine dog. Is he yours?" Benjy tried to speak, but it wasn't any use, so he just nodded his head. Coot then asked, "Is your daddy around?"

It was right then that Benjy was caught between lying and the truth, because he still didn't trust Coot's intention. He seemed harmless, and usually someone full of meanness didn't have any use for dogs or other animals. Had Benjy been blind he would not have felt any fear at all, but that wasn't the case. Benjy decided not to answer his question, but instead just asked, "Why do you want to see my papa?"

Coot raised up and smiled again. "Me and your daddy is hunting buddies." He stuck out his hand for Benjy to shake. "I'm Coot Hunter. I've done heard plenty about you from your daddy. You're Benjy, ain't you?"

Feeling about as dumb as a barrel of hair, Benjy dropped the hammer and crowbar. He was standing there shaking hands with the man he had been wanting to meet since the first time he had heard his papa telling one of Coot Hunter's famous hunting stories. Benjy's handshake was a weak one because he was now nervous about meeting the great legend for the first time. Benjy smiled and said, "I already know about you, too, Mr. Hunter. I've been listening to stories about you all my life."

Coot laid back his head and cackled aloud. Then he cocked his head and set that one bulging eye on Benjy and said, "Don't believe a word of what you hear unless you hear it from me, boy."

Benjy replied, "Yes sir, Mr. Hunter. I won't."

Then Coot cocked his head again like he couldn't talk with it straight up, and said, "Your daddy's done a good job of raisin' you, boy. And I reckon manners is a sign of respect for both the man receiving and the man giving. But my friends just call me Coot, and I'd appreciate it if you'd do me the honor."

Coot sure had a way of making a boy feel good

about himself. He had called Benjy a man and considered him a friend. Benjy said, "My papa has gone to town, but I think he'll back soon if you'd like to wait."

Coot reached up and took his hat from his head, revealing a tangled mess of hair that was in dire need of cutting. He then rubbed his forehead with his shirtsleeve and said, "I reckon sittin' here in the shade with good company beats pushing a wheelbarrow with rope handles in that hot sun." And then he seated himself on a bale of hay and spit out a wad of tobacco juice that would have drowned another man.

It was then a race between Benjy and Ole Blue to see who could get the best seat beside Coot, and Ole Blue won without any trouble at all. Coot started out with idle talk about Benjy's momma and papa being fine folks. Even though it was nice to hear him say good things about them, it wasn't what Benjy was wanting to hear. Finally Benjy said, "Coot, tell me a good hunting story. I hear you're the best storyteller and hunter in these parts."

Coot just smiled and said, "I thought you'd never ask." Benjy noticed that when he smiled his scar curled around his lips. "Well, boy, supposing you tell me which story is your favorite, and I'll tell it like you ain't never heard it before." Then he laid back his head and cackled again.

Benjy watched the scar jump up and down while Coot laughed. Even though the boy had been taught better than to question a man on personal matters, he was dying to know the story behind the scar. Benjy had heard all the rumors about Coot Hunter. But that's all they were—just rumors. No one knew for sure about Coot Hunter's scar or much else about him. It had been said that Coot got in a fight with a man years ago and ended up killing him. They said he was running from the law and hid in the woods and had been there ever since. Others said he had robbed a bank and buried the money in the woods, and he lived out there to protect it. But the story Benjy liked the best was the one where Coot barehanded took on a bobcat that had jumped his dog. They say he killed that cat with his hands, but not before it got his eye and face.

Benjy fidgeted a little because he was afraid of asking about the scar for fear Coot might be offended and leave. But as usual, curiosity got the best of him, and he said, "I ain't got a favorite story, Coot. But if you don't mind, I'd sure like to know how you got that scar on your face."

Coot's look went stone cold, and he reached up and ran a finger down the scar like he was remembering back on some awful memory. He didn't say a word, but just sat there staring off into space. Benjy was already sorry he had asked the question and he stuttered, "I . . . also like the story about you killing two deer with one shot. It's one of my favorites and you can tell me that one if you want."

But Coot's expression did not change, and he kept rubbing his scar like he didn't hear a word Benjy had

90

said. It was then that Benjy got a good look at the eye above the scar. It was a light blue color, and it had what looked like a white, milky cover over it. It wasn't pleasant to look at. The eye didn't move with the other one, and Benjy knew it wasn't any use to Coot. Him being blinded in one eye explained a lot of things, like why he cocked his head to one side, and why the other eye bulged out so much, and why Coot wore his hat pulled down to one side to cover it all. Benjy also noticed that the scar went straight to the eye, and he figured that whatever had caused that scar had gotten his eye, too.

Finally Coot let a click out of the corner of his mouth like he was calling up a horse and said, "Now, I reckon me killing two deer with one shot might sound a bit impossible, and I wouldn't believe it either if it was told by another man. But I know it to be true enough this once because I did it." Coot started telling his story, and it wasn't long until he was back to his old self. Benjy was glad for it, too. He felt bad about bringing back some bad memories for Coot. But Benjy didn't think about it again as he got caught up in the story. Coot didn't just sit and talk. He started acting out the motions like he was doing it all over again. He whooped and hollered and whispered in all the right places, and did like it was his first time to tell it. He even got Ole Blue to barking once or twice with his whoops, and it seemed as though Coot was enjoying his story as much as Benjy and Ole Blue, if that was possible.

He finished up his story, and Benjy was just before

begging for another one when he heard his papa drive up. Coot stood up, and once again shook Benjy's hand and thanked him for sitting with him and listening. Benjy was lost for words because he was the one who was supposed to be thanking Coot. His reply wasn't worth spit as he said, "I sure enjoyed the story." Those words didn't say the half of it.

Benjy watched as Coot walked to the door of the barn and then turned around and said what Benjy had been wishing for all his life. "I reckon me and you and your daddy is gonna have to get up a coon-hunting trip sometime soon. I'll talk to your daddy about it now." And then he pulled his hat good and tight down over his bad eye and with the bulging eye, gave Benjy a wink.

If it wasn't for good manners, Benjy would have been on his feet bothering both Coot and his papa until they agreed on a time to make that hunting trip. But his papa always said that begging was unnecessary and bothersome and not to be tolerated. So Benjy just sat there, squirming on the inside and out, like he did when one of his aunts started hugging on him.

Ole Blue followed Coot, and Benjy went as far as the barn door. He wanted to be in plain sight just in case his papa wanted his opinion on when would be a good time to make the trip. But all he got was a look from his papa, and both he and Coot were having a good laugh. Benjy saw his momma come out of the house and give Coot a couple of jars of whatever she had been canning. Coot took the jars and tipped his hat as a thank you.

After Coot left, Benjy's papa came to the barn and asked him, "Did Ole Coot give you a scare, boy?"

Benjy was embarrassed and felt foolish. He just answered back, "Papa, he sure is a sight to see, but when are we going on that hunting trip?"

His papa shook his head and said, "We'll see about that later."

Because his papa and Coot were friends, Benjy had the chance to get to know Coot better than most folks did. But he never found out the truth behind the scar because he never asked again. Maybe Coot kept silent because he really was running from the law, or maybe it was because it wasn't anybody's business. If something bad had happened in his past, Coot had learned from it and was sure making a good life for himself now. It didn't matter to Benjy. He liked not knowing the truth, because that's what made Coot mysterious and kept him a legend. But there was one truth Benjy knew about the man. Since his first encounter with him, there had never been a time that Benjy saw him as ugly or mean. Of all the things Coot taught him about hunting and life, there was one lesson that was more important than all the rest: You can't judge a person by his outward appearance. Because Coot had a good heart inside, he knew that's all a person should ever look for.

Benjy asked his grandpa once if he knew Coot

Hunter, because he was always wanting his grandpa's opinion on things. It was the only time Benjy could remember his grandpa having anything good to say about anyone from around these parts. He said, "To be honest with you, Benjy, I ain't met the man face-to-face, but I've heard all about him. A couple of winters ago when we had that hard, freezing weather, fresh meat was hard to come by. Folks couldn't get out and do much hunting, and I was one of them. But one morning, I went out on my front porch and there were two skinned squirrels laying there. I couldn't for the life of me figure out where they came from, but I was mighty glad to get them. Then about a week later, I heard a noise outside and I got up to see what it was, and there on the porch were two more squirrels. I saw someone walking down the road, and I don't know why I did it, but I hollered out Coot's name. He didn't turn around or stop but just took off his hat and gave it a wave and kept going."

Benjy asked, "Grandpa, how did you know it was Coot that was bringing you those squirrels?"

The old man just grinned and said, "Well, I reckon I put two and two together and came up with it. First, I knew it was a good hunter who was able to get out and kill fresh meat. And second, I reckon Coot, being an outcast like myself, he figured wouldn't anybody else be kind enough to do it for me. So he was the only one I could think of and I was right."

PART TWO:

Changes

CHAPTER THIRTEEN

When the Rabbits Don't Run

Benjy lost interest in school again while in the fifth grade. The only way he had made it this far was because of his momma's pushing and praying. There weren't many teachers like Mrs. Jones, and Benjy stayed lost and confused most of the time. He didn't know why, but it was so hard for him to learn. It made him care less and less about school. But there was another reason why Benjy's heart wasn't in his schoolwork, and that's because it was with Ole Blue.

Benjy didn't go to the woods much anymore except for hunting. The days of creek jumping and exploring were far and few between. Most of the adventure and excitement had been taken away, mainly because Benjy knew the woods like peanut butter knows jelly.

But he was also seeing changes in Ole Blue. Even though Ole Blue was up and ready at a slap on the hips, he just wasn't the same dog out in the woods. He went along mostly out of habit. Once in the woods, he didn't chase rabbits or scare up quail. Instead, he seemed content to stay at Benjy's side.

On days when Benjy was working around the house, Ole Blue just lay around sleeping. Most of the time, if Benjy threw a stick to be fetched, he'd just sort of whine and thump his tail as if to say, "I could, but I really don't want to." On the trips to deer camp, Ole Blue was right there, but he didn't do any hunting. And if he did, he didn't go far. That didn't bother Benjy much, because hunting wasn't one of Ole Blue's strong points. He was bred for it, having bluetick blood running through every vein, but Benjy had made him too much of a pet to be much good at hunting. He was still the best friend a boy could have. He had proved that more than once.

When Benjy first noticed Ole Blue slowing down, it worried him because he thought his dog was sick. But his papa gave Ole Blue a close inspection and then said, "Benjy, I can't find anything wrong with him except for the fact that he's getting old. You can't expect an old dog to act like a pup. If you give him a good rubdown every now and then, it will help to keep the blood flowing in his muscles, and he won't stay stiff and sore as much." Benjy knew his papa was right, and he started giving Ole Blue extra-special attention, which he took to like a bear to honey.

Every time Ole Blue saw Benjy coming, he would just roll over and lay out all four legs for Benjy to rub. He lay there with his eyes shut and grunted with every stroke.

At suppertime, Benjy started leaving scraps on his plate. It was unusual for him to leave anything behind, because his momma never excused him from the table until he had eaten all his food. She didn't believe in wasting food. She always said, "Waste not, want not." But now his momma knew that the extra food was for Ole Blue, and she never said a word.

All this special attention seemed to help, because through the fall, Ole Blue didn't get any worse. But in the winter things changed. The cold weather and rains didn't help, and Ole Blue stayed close to the house because he just couldn't get around much. Once, a neighbor, Mr. Tanner, made a visit to the house to discuss plans for the deer camp. And as they sat on the front porch, Ole Blue walked over to lie beside Benjy. Mr. Tanner noticed the dog and said, "Joe, that dog has seen his better days. You ought to do him a favor and take him out back and put him out of his misery."

Those were the cruelest words Benjy had ever heard from a man, and he was ready to put his good manners aside and tell Mr. Tanner a thing or two. But before Benjy got a chance, his papa set Mr. Tanner straight. He said, "If the dog was suffering any, I reckon you would be right, but the only thing that dog suffers from is too much love and attention.

I reckon he's been as good a dog as a boy could ask for, and if he's made it this long, I think he deserves that love in his old age."

Benjy looked at his papa and thanked him with his eyes, and Ole Blue started thumping his tail on the porch. Some folks said that dogs didn't understand much and relied on their instincts, but there was nothing wrong with Ole Blue's instinct or understanding. When Mr. Tanner got up to leave, Ole Blue let out a deep growl of warning, and Mr. Tanner jumped off the porch instead of using the steps where Benjy and his dog sat. Papa laughed and said, "I don't think Ole Blue likes your way of thinking in the least bit, Bill Tanner."

Mr. Tanner was embarrassed. He shook his head in agreement and replied, "I think you are right, and I also think Ole Blue is just the one to change my mind."

Benjy knew his dog couldn't live forever. Still, Blue's dying wasn't something he could force himself to think about. But the first time Benjy saw Ole Blue leave his feed bowl half-full, he knew that it wasn't going to be long. If a dog had to be extra good at something, eating was it for Ole Blue. Benjy once again asked his papa to get a vet, but he just said, "Son, there ain't a thing a vet can do for old age."

The very next night at feeding time, Ole Blue just took a sniff at his feed bowl and put his head back down. Benjy did everything he knew to do, short of eating the food for him, but it wasn't any use. As

Benjy lay in bed that night, he did what any body would do to try and save his dog. He promised the Good Lord everything he owned, including a Christian life that would make the angels sing, if He would just let Ole Blue live.

Some time late in the night, Benjy went outside to check on Ole Blue and found him curled up in his favorite spot in the barn. He thumped his tail as a sign of life, and Benjy lowered the lamp light and sat down beside him. Ole Blue laid his head in Benjy's lap, and the boy gave his dog every reason in the world why he should keep on living and not give up. Tears rolled down his cheeks with every word. When Benjy got up to leave, Ole Blue whimpered low, and that was all Benjy could take. He put the lantern out and lay down with his dog in the hay. He put one arm under Ole Blue's head and the other across his body. Even though there was a nip of cold in the air, Benjy was as warm as his momma's oven as he went to sleep.

The sun was just before breaking when Benjy woke the next morning. Ole Blue was still alive, but he was breathing heavy, and his ribs were sucking in and out with each breath. Benjy tried to get him to eat, but Ole Blue wouldn't even sniff at the food. He just lay there and looked at Benjy with his big brown eyes as if he were saying, "It ain't no use. I'm just not up to it anymore."

Benjy went inside and scared his momma when she saw him coming in from the porch. He told her that

Ole Blue wouldn't make it through the day. His momma just said, "Son, I wish there was something I could do for him and you both, but there isn't." And then she gave him a long hug. Benjy and his momma cried again for what they knew was coming. His momma wiped her eyes and said, "Ain't no need in you going to school today. Your place is here with your dog."

His papa came into the kitchen, and Benjy told him about Ole Blue. He didn't say anything with words, but instead gave Benjy a comforting pat on the back. They all sat down and ate a quiet breakfast, but Benjy was feeling as bad as Ole Blue, and his eggs might as well have been green beans because he couldn't eat a bite. His papa got up to leave for work, and Benjy fixed two biscuits for Ole Blue. As he went out on the front porch, Benjy saw his papa coming from the barn, and he was wiping his eyes as he climbed into his truck and left. Benjy had never thought about it before, but Ole Blue wasn't just special to him alone. He knew his papa had been in the barn thanking Ole Blue for all the things he had done for their family and for keeping a good watchful eye on his boy in the past years.

Benjy took the biscuits out to the barn, but he was too late. Ole Blue had taken his last breath. Benjy lay down beside him and cried again until his dog's head and floppy ears were soaked with tears. He buried Ole Blue beneath an old oak beside the house. It was one of his favorite spots in the summertime because it was shady and cool, and there always seemed to be a breeze there. Benjy wrapped Ole Blue in an old blanket from the barn and buried him with the two biscuits. He made a cross and put it on top of the grave as he said a prayer for his dog. Then Benjy got up and started walking toward the woods. But just as he reached the edge of the field, he turned and walked back to the house. He couldn't force himself to go into the woods alone. He wasn't sure if he would ever be able to again.

Benjy decided to go to his grandpa's house. He needed to get away because everything he did and everywhere he looked, he was reminded of his dog. His grandpa was very understanding, and they drove into town and ate lunch at the cafe. Benjy knew this was a rare occasion because his grandpa only shopped at the general store and only because he had to for supplies. It was also the first time Benjy had seen his grandpa around people other than family, and there was quite a difference. Folks turned and stared as the two sat down at a table. Benjy noticed his grandpa's nervousness and agitation as the old man wiped his forehead with his handkerchief.

Finally a waitress came over to take their order. The old man never looked up as he spoke and his voice was harsh like he was being bothered. Benjy was embarrassed by his grandpa's rudeness to the woman, and he turned his head and began watching the others in the cafe. A few of the older men were drinking coffee and talking in low voices. Every now and then they would cut their eyes over to look at his grandpa. Benjy was quite sure they were talking about him and the old man, and he began to feel uncomfortable, too. The food was served and the both of them hurriedly ate and left the cafe.

His grandpa insisted that they shop around at the general store before leaving, and he bought Benjy a new hunting vest. For a while Benjy forgot his pain over Ole Blue's dying. But on the way home, he wanted to talk about it and he said, "Grandpa, I miss Ole Blue, and I don't think I'll ever get over this." Just saying his dog's name brought a lump in his throat.

His grandpa rubbed his old whiskers and stared out the window. "I don't think anybody ever gets over losing someone they love." His grandpa's voice was lonesome and sad as he continued. "It changes your life and you do things that you wish . . ." He didn't finish what he was saying. Benjy knew his grandpa was talking about his wife, because she was the only person his grandpa had ever lost, or at least the only one Benjy knew about. His grandpa quickly changed the subject back to Ole Blue. "Time will help you, Benjy. In time it will get easier to talk about Ole Blue and easier to remember him without any pain."

Benjy was feeling better as his grandpa dropped him off at the road to his house. But with each step he took closer to home, he was reminded of Ole Blue. He couldn't remember a time in his life when he had made that walk alone, and right then it felt like only half of him was walking the road. It was a lonely feeling that cut him deep and he doubted his grandpa's word.

Benjy went straight for Ole Blue's grave, and the first thing he saw from a distance was a small bunch of flowers planted neatly beneath the cross. Benjy knew his momma had been there, and it warmed his heart. All along Benjy had been thinking on how lucky he was to have such a good dog, but he also realized Ole Blue was pretty lucky too, to have a family that loved him back just as much.

A month or so passed by, and his grandpa was right about it getting easier to remember Old Blue without so much hurting. But there wasn't one morning that he didn't walk out of his house and look for Ole Blue just the same as he had done every day for the past ten years. He wasn't sure if it was habit or hope that made him do it, but he did it just the same. Benjy could hardly eat a buttered biscuit, and he hated taking the supper scraps outside in the evening.

Then one afternoon, Mr. Tanner made another stop by the house. He climbed out of the truck and greeted Benjy and his papa who were sitting on the front porch. He still wasn't Benjy's favorite person because of what he had said about Ole Blue.

Mr. Tanner motioned at Benjy and said, "Come here, boy. I got something I want to show you." Benjy looked at his papa who had a grin on his face that said he knew something, but he wasn't telling it. Benjy got up and went to the truck bed and looked over to where Mr. Tanner was pointing. What he saw made his heart jump. It was the tiniest little pup he had ever seen, and it was the spitting image of Ole Blue. Benjy jumped into the truck quick as a cat and held the pup in his arms. He checked him over from head to toe, and the pup was marked in every way like Ole Blue. Mr. Tanner was laughing and said, "What's the matter, boy? Are you checking to see if he's real or not?"

Benjy was still in shock. "I can't believe he looks so much like my dog, Ole Blue."

Mr. Tanner said, "Yeah, it looks like Ole Blue was still getting around pretty good some four months ago. I guess there's some things you never get too old for."

Everyone laughed, including Benjy, as he thought about Ole Blue being so old and having a girlfriend. Then Mr. Tanner said, "There were eight of these pups, and when I saw your daddy in town some time ago, he told me your dog had died. I told him about the pups, and he asked if I'd bring one to you when they were weaned."

Benjy's momma came out on the porch and joined her husband. They both were grinning at Benjy and quite proud of themselves for having kept such a good secret. Benjy thanked Mr. Tanner and climbed out of the truck. He put the puppy on the ground and then whistled as he slapped his leg and said, "Come on, Blue Jr., come on, boy." The little pup just swished his little whip of a tail at Benjy and followed his footsteps as they walked to the barn.

CHAPTER FOURTEEN

A Day of Reckoning

There's a big difference between knowing you're dumb and the rest of the world knowing it, too. You can cover it up by being lazy and making excuses, and pretty soon you get lost in the crowd. If you act as though you don't care, that's the way you get treated, and Benjy had learned this was the easy way to not get noticed. He knew the truth, and as long as no one else knew it, he could accept it. But in the sixth grade that all changed, and if a boy had a turning point in his schooling, this was it.

It was a gradual happening. Benjy just didn't wake up one morning feeling dumb. But there came a time when he began to notice that he wasn't as smart as everyone else, and no matter how hard he tried, it wasn't going to change. All of his teachers would stand before the class with number cards, and each time they would flash a new card at the class, Benjy wasn't fast enough to answer with the rest of the kids. He thought that even if he had all day to answer, it wouldn't matter. He didn't know the answer and never would.

This was mostly true with numbers. They were always confusing, because about the time he recognized the numbers, the signs would change from adding to subtracting. And the worst part was when he tried to divide and multiply. Even when Benjy worked at home by himself, it took him a long time to do his work, only to find out that he was still getting only half of the problems right.

And it was the same way with reading and writing. He would listen to other kids reading in class, and the words rolled off their tongues as smooth as hair on a frog's back. If Benjy knew ahead of time that he would be reading in front of the class, he would take his reader home and practice with his momma. She would help him through the stories, saying the words her son didn't know. When they were finished, she always told Benjy that he had done well. But Benjy knew differently. His momma had just never heard the other kids read. And all his practicing didn't help much. When it was Benjy's turn to read, it was the same spitting and sputtering, and he still needed help from the teacher on the same words he had trouble with the night before. It wasn't long until his teacher and probably everyone else in class knew that Benjy couldn't read very well. Because of this, he wasn't called on much to read anymore.

Benjy didn't mind though. It was easier to sit back and listen to the stories. Even though reading wasn't his best subject, he still liked it better than the rest. There was life in the stories that held his fascination. Sometimes he would sit back and close his eyes and imagine the characters as they went through their adventures, and it was like he was a part of the tale being told.

But then something happened. Benjy's teacher sent word to his momma that she wanted to see her. Benjy didn't know the reason behind it, but he had a hard time convincing his momma. She thought her son had been misbehaving at school, and even though Benjy told her it wasn't true, she worried and fretted just the same. She even told Benjy if he was lying, she would whip him double for it. She had Benjy wanting to admit to things he hadn't done, just in case something had slipped his mind.

His papa caught a ride to the woods one day, and his momma drove the truck to school. Benjy saw her coming down the hall after school and she looked as nervous as he had been on his first day. She was holding tight to her purse much like he had done with his lunch sack on that day. When she saw her son, she frowned as if expecting the worst. "Where can I find your teacher, Benjy?" He pointed to the door, and they both walked in. His teacher tried to calm his momma by offering her a chair. Then the teacher said, "Benjy, would you mind waiting outside while I talk to your mother?" Benjy didn't like the idea. If they were going to be talking about him, he wanted to be there to defend himself. But his momma motioned him out the door like a bothersome fly.

As he left the room, he pulled the door to, but not shut, so he could still hear what was being said. After the meeting was over, he wished he hadn't done it. It was then that his momma found out that he wasn't smart and probably wouldn't be no matter how hard he tried. And even though Benjy knew this, it was like his teacher was pulling his dumbness out of him for the whole world to see. He was leaning against the wall, and it was like every word his teacher said was pounding him as he slid down the wall into a squatting position. He laid his head in his arms with shame. It wasn't every day a boy had to face up to the truth that he was dumber than everybody else and listen while his momma was being told the same thing.

Benjy thought back to his first day at school when he had told Miss Grider that he was already smart enough and didn't need to go to school. He remembered walking out of the room after Miss Grider had laughed at him. If he had known this day was going to take place, he would never have gone back.

His momma came out of the room and gave him a smile and offered her hand to help him up. She gave his hand a little squeeze and then let it drop as they walked out of the schoolhouse together. Benjy felt awkward and afraid as they drove home. He didn't know what to say, but his momma eased his mind, and it turned out to be a nice ride after all. They talked about the sweet smell of honeysuckle and how pretty spring days were compared to the dead of winter. His momma said, "Spring is a time of new life. It's Mother Nature's way of saying we've survived another winter and everything is going to be fine." And then she smiled and reached over and patted her son on the shoulder and said, "I love you, son." And Benjy knew that this was his momma's way of saying that everything was, indeed, going to be fine.

And even though his momma never mentioned it again, Benjy was not the same boy. There wasn't any use in trying to cover it up. All the extra hours of practicing his math and reading weren't worth spit if dumb was dumb, or at least that's the way he saw it. Knowing he was different seemed to set him apart from the other kids. No one was mean to him, but it was like he couldn't find a place to fit in with the others. When they went outside to play games, he was the last one to get picked for a team, if he even decided to play. Most of the time, he just watched.

After that day, he wasn't called on to do much in class, either. It seemed as though any attempt at his work was good enough, and his teacher didn't bother him anymore. It was like she knew he was dumb, and there wasn't any need of expecting much from a dumb kid.

Benjy had decided that in another year he would be old enough to start going to the woods with his papa and learn the logging business. One night at the supper table, he mentioned his idea, and it was the last time he made that mistake. Supper lasted a long time that night. By the time his momma and papa finished talking, he knew that no matter how dumb he was, he was going to get his diploma and graduate. His momma said she would die seeing to it, but it would happen. And Benjy knew she meant it, too.

But the man who really gave Benjy the courage to face up to himself and not give up on learning was his grandpa. Benjy wasn't one to hide his feelings very well, and he had been moping around for about a month. Finally, one day when he turned down the chance to go fishing, the old man asked, "Boy, what in the world is the matter with you? You haven't been yourself for days now."

Benjy didn't want to talk about it, because the last person he wanted to know about his being dumb was his grandpa. It was bad enough that his momma and papa knew, and that's where he wanted his secret to stay. But the old man didn't give up when he received no answer. "Boy, whatever it is, it's best to get it off your chest. Keeping a problem inside just makes things worse. It's like a sore inside of you.

It won't go away until you tend to it."

His words made sense to Benjy, and he then realized he was wanting to talk about it more than he thought. It was hard to find the right words to explain what he was feeling, but finally he said, "Grandpa, I ain't doing so good in school, and no matter how hard I try, it won't matter. I won't ever get any better at it. I'm just dumb."

His grandpa cocked his head to one side and frowned in disbelief. "Boy, you ain't dumb. You figure things out that a grown man spends a lifetime trying to learn. I ain't believing what I'm hearing."

Benjy was more confused than ever. It made him feel good to hear his grandpa say those things about him, but at the same time, it made him feel bad. "Grandpa, figuring things out for myself doesn't seem to matter a hoot when it comes to reading and writing and arithmetic. I don't get A's on my card for thinking. It doesn't seem to matter to my teacher, either. We don't study 'figuring things out' in school. Least way, we haven't studied it yet."

His grandpa rubbed the back of his neck and then gave his whiskers a stroke or two, like he always did when he was thinking. Then he said, "I see what you're saying now, boy. I guess there is a big difference, but I ain't sure which one is more important." He then stopped and got out of his rocker and seated himself beside Benjy on the steps of the porch. He continued, "I ain't sure if what I'm about to say is going to make much sense to you, but I'm going to

say it anyway, because I think you need to hear it."
Benjy's head was hanging as low as his spirits, but
he listened like a man in need of salvation. "There's
two kinds of learning in this world, Benjy. There's
learning about life and how to be a good man and
how to think for yourself, and there's book learning,
which opens up doors to let you be a doctor or a
lawyer or work in a bank. It gives you a chance to
choose what you want to be. I guess it would be
perfect if you had both, but sometimes it doesn't work
that way." The old man stopped to see if his grandson
was understanding, and Benjy nodded his head.
"Well, the way I see it, you've been blessed in one
area and not so blessed in the other. But that doesn't
make you dumb. It just makes you different. And
being different ain't nothing to be ashamed of."

Benjy looked up at his grandpa. "Well, I don't see
any sense in staying in school if I can't learn anything.
I don't guess I'll ever be a doctor or a lawyer or work
in a bank. The way I see it, I should just stop going
to school and go to work with papa in the woods. I'll
probably end up being a logger like my papa, anyway."

The old man quickly replied, "You've got it all
wrong, Benjy. You've been in school six years now,
and you know how to read and you know how to
write and you can do some adding and subtracting.
You may not be as good at it as the rest of your class,
but you still know how to do it. If you've learned that
much in six years, just think what you might learn in

114

the next six years if you stay in school. You're giving up too easy, and I know you to be more stubborn than that."

As his grandpa rubbed his head, Benjy smiled on the inside as well as the outside. It was the first time in a long time that he felt good about himself. He said, "Grandpa, I think you're right. I just never thought about it that way. How did you get so smart?"

The old man looked into his grandson's face as he said, "From years of doing things the wrong way, boy, and Lord knows I've had my share of that."

CHAPTER FIFTEEN

The Fire Is Rekindled

It was Benjy's grandpa that got him interested in school again, but it was Miss Potter, his seventh-grade teacher, who set him on fire with a burning desire to learn. She was a storyteller who could give Coot Hunter a run for his money anytime, and she never let a day go by that she didn't read to her class. But it wasn't just ordinary reading that she did. She would lay her book in front of her, and it was like the story was inside her and just dying to get out when she began her reading.

As she read, the whole class would sit on the edge of their seats in great anticipation and awe of her performance. And just when she got to the good part, she would say, "And if you want to know how the story ends, you'll have to read it yourself." It didn't matter how much moaning and groaning and begging the class did; she wouldn't read another word. And because of this, Benjy took his reader home every night. It took him a while to do it, but he finished every story Miss Potter started.

But it didn't stop there. The next day in class, Miss Potter would ask her students what they thought about the story. It took Benjy a long time to get up the nerve to say anything in front of the other boys and girls, because he had gotten used to sitting back and hiding his dumbness. But Miss Potter wasn't one to allow that, and once she saw what Benjy was doing, she started to call on him to talk. At first, Benjy would just shrug his shoulders and say he didn't know, even though that wasn't the truth. But Miss Potter didn't allow that, either. She would say, "You have an opinion, don't you, Mr. King? You have a brain and it thinks, doesn't it?" She always called everybody "Mr." and "Miss" and it made her students feel all grown-up and big, like they should have an opinion even if they didn't. So it wasn't long before Benjy was raising his hand to talk, before Miss Potter had a chance to call on him. And no matter what he said, she always had something good to say about his opinions.

And somehow, Benjy improved in his writing too, because sometimes Miss Potter would make her students write down their opinions first and then read them aloud in class. Benjy's writing wasn't the best, but knowing he had something to say made it easier to do.

His biggest challenge came when Miss Potter assigned her students to write their own stories and read them in front of the class. Benjy wanted to do the best of anybody in class, but it seemed as though his brain had become as blank as an opossum's stare while playing dead. Benjy told his papa about the assignment, and his papa came up with the perfect story. It was a true story, and Benjy didn't have any trouble writing it. And the reading part was easier too, because the story really was inside of him, dying to get out. Benjy had two of the best storytellers as examples to follow, and once he got before the class and told his story, even Coot would have been proud of his performance. Benjy's story was about his first coon-hunting trip that he had been promised by Coot and his papa.

He was nervous at first, but once he got started, he became as comfortable as a rocking chair after a long day of work. And this is the story he told.

Coot Hunter is a legend in this county because of his great hunting ability. The first time I ever had the pleasure of meeting him, he made a promise to take me coon-hunting. The day finally came to make this trip and I spent all afternoon preparing myself for the hunt. I strapped all my hunting stuff on me, and when I came out of the house that evening, I could hardly walk because I was so loaded down. Coot took one look at me and laid back his head and let out one of his famous hunting calls and almost laughed himself to death. He said to me, "Boy, you look funnier than a rooster wearing socks. We're going hunting for one night, not a whole week." My papa, who was going on the trip with us, just smiled and helped me to untie everything that was attached.

We loaded up in Coot's truck, and even though my dog, Ole Blue, wasn't exactly fond of being tied up in the back with all Coot's dogs, I finally got him tied in. It wasn't long until Coot started in on one of his famous tales about a coon hunt, and I listened to every word, hoping to learn something before I got my chance to experience my first coon hunt. Coot pointed out the window to a tree stump that was sitting out in a pond about six feet above water. He said, "You see that ole stump, boy? Well, a couple of winters ago, I was out hunting around that pond, which was frozen solid. I guess I'd been hunting there for about three nights straight, and every night my redbone hound, Ole Lightnin', had been outsmarted by this coon. It was something my dog wasn't use to, and every night about dusk, he'd start barking and baying to go back after that coon. It being cold and all, I wasn't really wanting to go out that night, but Ole Lightnin' would let out a bawl that sent shivers up and down me, and I guess it got my blood to boiling, so I loaded him up and headed back to that pond.

"It wasn't long that night before Ole Lightnin'

caught hold of that coon's scent and he was hot on his trail. I was whooping and hollering, and clear across on the other side of the pond, I saw that big coon running across the ice and heading for that stump. Ole Lightnin' was right behind him, and if it hadn't been for the ice, he would have gotten him, too. But as it was, my dog couldn't get a good footing, and he was doing more sliding than running. I couldn't help myself, and I laid back and laughed at the sight before me. Once I got my light back on the chase, I watched as Ole Lightnin' jumped and caught that coon halfway up that stump. I guess it was the jump that caused the ice to break, and the next thing I knew, my dog and that coon were both down in the water, fighting for their lives. That coon was trying to get on top of Lightnin's head, and it scared me for fear that he would drown my dog. So like a fool, I went running across the ice, slipping like Ole Lightnin' had done, but this time, it wasn't near as funny.

"Well, by the time I reached the stump, my dog and that coon had declared war on one another, and it was a real toss-up as to who was going to win. I saw Lightnin' put that coon under, and when he came up, that coon would return the favor and give Lightnin' a good dunking. I took a couple steps closer, which was a mistake on my part, and the next thing I knew, the ice gave way and I was right between the two of them. That icy water hit me about neck high, and I thought for sure I would be found the next morning in a box of ice. The only thing I could think about was to break up the fight and get myself and Lightnin' back to safety. I grabbed my dog by the collar, and that coon by the nape of his neck, figuring on separating the two and giving that coon a free shot to run. But it seemed that the both of them had a different idea, and between the two of them, they managed to send me clear to the bottom of that pond. I came up screaming bloody murder, and I guess it scared the both of them, because that coon jumped to the stump and then made a diving leap to the other side. He hit on that ice and was gone before Lightnin' had a chance to know what was happening. If I hadn't grabbed my dog's collar again, he would have been right on his trail, too. But as far as I was concerned, that coon could live forever, because I knew if we didn't get out of that ice water soon, we would both be dead.

"I finally got the two of us back on solid ice, and darn if Lightnin' didn't take out across the pond again, still trailing that coon. As for me, I just crawled across the ground, praying to God to let me get to my truck. I stripped down to the bare and drove home, naked as a newborn baby. Sometime later that night, I finally thawed out beside my potbellied stove. As for Lightnin', I guess he spent the rest of the night chasing that coon. In the morning, I walked out and there he was on the front porch, covered with ice and sound asleep."

By the time Coot finished his story, I was tired and worn out, like I had already gone through one hunting trip. I asked Coot if he and Lightnin' ever got that coon, and he just laughed and said, "I learned a long time ago that if the Good Lord sees fit to spare your life once, don't be fool enough to test His kindness a second time."

As the truck started slowing down, I felt myself getting anxious again about the hunting we were going to do. That story Coot told had wet my whistle for a hunt, and I was ready to prove to both Coot and my papa that I was old enough and ready to be a full-fledged coon hunter. They turned the dogs loose and then sat back on the tailgate, waiting for the first treeing bark. It didn't take long, and even though I didn't recognize the bark, I knew it was time to go when Coot and my papa started yelling out encouragement to the barking dog.

Coot said, "It's my dog, Ole Tater, and she's treed a coon. Let's go." We started out through the woods, and it wasn't long until we came up on Tater, and I saw her stretched high on the trunk of a big oak. The dog had a deep baying voice, and it was like music in the night. Coot shined his light into the tree, and we finally spotted that coon out on the tip end of a long branch. Coot said, "Good girl, Tater. You've treed a fine coon."

I was waiting for Coot or Papa to fire up a shot and bring the coon down, but neither one of them raised their guns. I should have known right then and there that something fishy was going on, but it being my first coon hunt, I didn't say anything. I saw Coot and Papa exchange looks and then Coot said, "I sure wish that coon would jump and give Tater another chance to tree him. She's a young dog and the experience would do her good."

My papa sort of grinned and said, "It's real important to start a young dog out right, but if we shoot the coon, I guess it won't go far, and Tater's sure to catch it if it hits the ground."

Coot nodded in agreement and then replied, "What we need is some way to get that coon out of that tree and running again. I guess I could climb up there and give that limb a good shaking, but I'm getting a little too old to climb trees anymore."

I saw this as my chance to prove myself as a coon hunter and I said, "I ain't too old to climb up there if you would give me a boost to that first limb."

Coot and Papa again looked at each other, and I saw the both of them roll their tongues around as though they were trying hard to swallow the grins on their faces. Then my papa said, "I don't know, Benjy. It's mighty dangerous business climbing trees in the night. You might get hurt."

That made me want to go up that tree even more, and I said, "Papa, you know I can climb any tree in this county blindfolded. I won't get hurt."

Coot said, "Let the boy go up. He'll be all right."

Of course, my papa gave in, and they both gave me a lift up the tree and then stood below, shining the light for me to see. Once I was straddled across the limb with the coon on it, I heard Coot holler up, "Now crawl out to that coon, and once you're as close as you can get, give that limb a good shaking."

123

I scooted out as far as I could and then hollered back, "Is this far enough?"

Coot yelled back, "Get a little closer if you can."

It was about that time that Coot's light hit upon that coon, and what I saw staring back at me was the meanest and biggest red-eyed varmint in the county. I didn't scoot one inch closer either, but instead started shaking that limb with all the strength I had in me. I was hoping to get rid of that coon as quick as I could. I didn't want Coot or my papa to know it, but it wasn't at all enjoyable being out on that limb with that coon. As soon as I stopped shaking the limb, that coon started snarling and growling and showed me a set of teeth that made me die on the inside. I saw that coon take two steps toward me, and I was just before jumping when the light went out. I was left up in that tree in total darkness with a snarling coon that had no plans of leaving.

I was no longer worried about what my papa or Coot thought about me being afraid. I was scared to the bone as I hollered down, "Get that light on me! I think this coon is coming to get me!"

But the only reply I got was roars of laughter from down below. Coot and my papa both yelled back, "Get 'em, boy. Don't let that coon get away. Shake him out of there."

I scooted back a ways and shook that limb once more until I thought it would break. But it didn't faze that coon in the least bit. The more I shook, the madder I made him. And with every scoot I took

124

backwards, that coon took two steps toward me. I was screaming, Tater was barking, and Coot and my papa were having themselves a good rib-busting laugh. I looked below once and saw the outline of them both, and they were doubled over and holding their sides. If that coon hadn't been my main concern at the time, I sure would have been looking for something to throw at the both of them. I wasn't wanting to give up, but I knew if a coon would take on a man and his dog in icy water, he sure wasn't going to give in to me, especially with me sitting straddle a limb in the dark and screaming my fool head off. Once more I hollered down for the light, but it wasn't any use. I guess it was then that I caught on that my being up in that tree, with a coon ready to scratch my eyeballs out, didn't have a thing to do with giving Tater a second chance to tree. So I didn't waste any time nor spare any of my skin getting down out of there.

Once I hit the ground, Coot and my papa managed to gain enough control of their laughing to ask, "What's the matter, boy? You ain't got that coon down yet. Get back up there and give him one more shake. That coon is sure to give in this time."

I looked the both of them dead in the eyes and said, "If the Good Lord sees fit to spare your life once, don't be fool enough to test His kindness a second time."

That was the end of Benjy's story, and when he was finished, the whole class started clapping, and he thought Miss Potter was going to hug his neck. She stood up and was clapping her hands above her head and yelling, "Bravo! Bravo!" Benjy didn't know exactly what she was saying, but he remembered his worst day at school, when his momma found out he wasn't as smart as the rest. And now he had his best day proving that it wasn't true.

CHAPTER SIXTEEN

The Saving Day

Benjy had been raised believing that religion was just as important as eating and sleeping. But sometimes around noon on Sunday, when Preacher Wilson was just getting his second wind and Benjy was getting hungry, he had a hard time believing that preaching and eating were equal. The only thing that saved him from a whole afternoon of preaching was the fact that Preacher Wilson was a big man with a big appetite. He used to joke with the menfolk of the church by saying, "I wasn't born a Baptist, but my momma said I enjoyed eating too much to be anything else." Benjy had been attending church ever since he was a baby, but attending and paying attention were two different things. He didn't understand much of what was going on or being said when he was younger, but all that changed during the summer after his eighth grade year of school.

Preacher Wilson got Benjy's attention when he spent a whole month preaching on hellfire and the damnation of the soul. He had Benjy scared and thinking of this hellfire business quite a bit, and Benjy finally decided the best thing to do was talk to his papa about it. He waited until they were alone in the barn and feeding the cows. Then he said, "Papa, does it scare you when Preacher Wilson starts talking about hellfire and damnation?"

His papa stopped doing his chores and leaned his pitchfork against the barn wall. He then turned a bucket upside down and took a seat. He looked his son in the eyes and said, "You don't have to be scared of hellfire and the devil if you're filled with the Holy Spirit, son."

Benjy knew what being filled with the Holy Spirit meant because Miss Mattie Johnson, a lady in the church, got filled with it at least once a month and sometimes even more. Benjy had heard his papa talking with some of the other men of the church one time, and they said they could always tell whether Preacher Wilson had delivered a good sermon because Miss Mattie was either sound asleep or up shouting and dancing.

Benjy picked up a straw of hay and started to chew on it. He didn't know why, but he was very nervous. "Papa," he asked, "Is getting filled with the Holy

Spirit like what happens to Miss Mattie when she starts dancing and shouting in the aisles?"

His papa sort of grinned and then quickly hid his smile behind his hand. "Well, yes and no. Most of the time Miss Mattie just gets excited, but if she wasn't filled with the Holy Spirit, I don't guess she would have anything to get excited about." His papa stopped a minute and then asked, "Benjy, is something bothering you?"

His question made Benjy even more flustered. "No, sir . . . there ain't nothing bothering me. . . ." He looked at his papa and then away again. "Well, I guess there is one thing I've been thinking about."

His papa had a serious look on his face. "What is it, boy?"

Benjy was kicking at the dirt on the barn floor, and his throat was as dry as the dust he was stirring up. "Well, I just don't want to die and go to hell. I'm pretty sure it's time for me to be saved and baptized."

His papa's face was full of pride, and he stood up and gave his son a strong hug. Then he said, "I'm proud of you, son. I've been waiting a long time to hear you say those words. I guess we'll need to take a ride down to Preacher Wilson's house after we finish the chores." He gave his son another hug and said, "You finish up here while I go speak to your momma."

Benjy and his momma and papa went to Preacher Wilson's house later that evening, and he helped

Benjy to understand what being saved meant and then it happened. Down on his knees, Benjy prayed that the Good Lord would save his soul, and in return, he promised to live a life He would always be proud of. Benjy knew when it happened, because he felt safe and warm on the inside, like the Good Lord had put His arms around him.

His momma cried on the way home because she was so happy for her son. Benjy felt good about being saved and looked forward to being baptized down at the river on Sunday. He knew this was an important day in his life, and he wanted his grandpa to be there. But he also knew how his momma and papa felt about him, so he was scared when he said, "Papa, I want Grandpa to come to church with us on Sunday and see me get baptized."

His papa's face went stone cold and he got really serious. "Benjy, I don't think that's a good idea. Your grandpa is not welcome in our church. He won't be able to come."

Benjy hadn't been saved long, and maybe he didn't understand everything he was supposed to, but it didn't seem right to him that a church should be shutting the doors to anybody. The Good Lord had just forgiven him for all his sins, and the way he had it figured, he and every other saved person could do the same for his grandpa. He argued, "Papa, it ain't right for the church to keep Grandpa out. Ain't we supposed to be inviting folks to come to church instead of asking them not to?"

His momma started to say something, but his papa quickly interrupted her. "Benjy, you're as right as rain on a dying crop, but there's something you don't understand. Your grandpa ain't wanted in the church because that's the way he wants it. People have gone to visit him before, and he's not very warm and inviting. He wouldn't come if you asked him to your baptism, so it's just a waste of time."

But Benjy didn't believe that. He just knew that whatever he asked of his grandpa, he would do for him. "But I can ask him, can't I? And if he says yes, will the church let him come in?"

Again his momma started to say something, and again his papa stopped her. Benjy could tell by the look on his momma's face that she was angry about not getting her say in. And he also knew that before the night was over his papa would hear it, whether he wanted to or not. His papa kept his eyes on the road and then said, "You can ask him if you want to, but if he turns you down and it hurts your feelings, don't blame me, because I tried to tell you so." This time his momma didn't have a thing to say, but instead just turned her head and glared an angry stare out the window.

Benjy was up early the next morning so he could get his chores done and go tell his grandpa the good news. His momma didn't ask him where he was going when he left because she knew.

Benjy and Blue Jr. didn't waste any time getting over to his grandpa's house, and they found him sitting in his rocker on the front porch, as usual. His grandpa didn't get around much anymore, and a lot of the time, Benjy's visits were more for helping him with his chores than just for good company. But it didn't matter to the old man why his grandson came. He was always glad to see him, and Benjy had thought on more than one occasion, it was because his grandpa was getting lonely in his old age.

The old man didn't get up to greet his grandson anymore because getting up and down was a challenge. But he sure could light up and make Benjy feel as welcome as ice water on a hot day. Benjy jumped up on the porch and gave his grandpa his usual hug, and then bent over so his grandpa could give his head a good rubbing. Then his grandpa said, "What brings you over so early, boy? Are you wanting to do some serious fishing this morning?" His voice was coarse and rough, and Benjy knew the old man had been through a long night of coughing. The boy had spent the night with him some lately, and some nights, the coughing was worse than others.

Benjy seated himself in the cane-bottom chair next to his grandpa's rocker and propped his elbows on his knees. "Grandpa, I got something I want to tell you and something I want to ask you." Benjy was excited and it showed in his voice.

The old man smiled a big, toothless grin and said, "I already know what it is. You're getting married, and you want me to dance at your wedding." Before Benjy had time to answer him back, he said, "Well, in my opinion, you're too young to get married, and I'm certainly too old to dance anymore. But if you're willing, so am I." The old man was proud of himself for getting the best of his grandson, and he laid back his head and laughed good and hard.

Benjy laughed too, but it wasn't because of what he had said. It was because he was having such a good time saying it. He was old, but still as sharp as a whip's crack. Benjy said, "Grandpa, I ain't getting married, but something real important is going to happen to me and I want you to be there."

The old man still had a grin on his face, but the laughing had stopped. "What is it, boy? What are you up to now?"

Benjy cracked his knuckles in nervousness and then said, "Well, my momma and papa took me over to Preacher Wilson's house last night, and I was saved. I guess me and the Good Lord got things right between us, and I'm real happy about it." Benjy watched the old man closely as he talked, and he saw his grin slowly disappear from his face. He didn't want to give his grandpa a chance to say anything until he asked him the final question. "Grandpa, I'm going to be baptized down at the river on Sunday, and I want you to be there."

Benjy was hoping the old man would just agree to it and be happy for him, but it didn't happen that way. His grandpa turned his head and stared off in the other direction, as if Benjy wasn't there. It was a long time before either one of them spoke again.

Benjy was too scared and the old man was thinking. Finally his grandpa said, "Benjy, I think it's real good that you got saved and I'm glad about it. But I ain't coming to your baptism. I don't guess there's any love lost between me and that Baptist church. I don't allow them to come to my house, and I ain't going to theirs. I don't aim to hurt you none, but this is just one time I'm going to have to say no to you."

Benjy could not believe what he was hearing. It was just as his papa said it would be, and it didn't make any sense to him. Instead, it made him mad and it hurt his feelings. He was tired of not knowing why things were so bad between his grandpa and everybody else who knew him. He had been told once to leave it alone and not ask questions, but he was a young boy then. Now it was different and he wanted to know the truth. "Grandpa, what in the world is going on? Everybody in this town has got something against you, and I guess I've heard every reason for it. You have your version. Momma and Papa have got theirs. But nobody is telling me the truth. At least it never feels like the truth. Whatever it is, it must be pretty bad if it would keep you from coming to see me get baptized." Benjy hesitated and waited for a reply, but the old man remained silent. His silence made Benjy even angrier and he said, "If this wasn't important to me, I wouldn't be asking you to come. But it is important and I want you there."

Benjy stood up and faced the old man. He wanted the truth this time, and he wasn't going to stop until he got it. But his grandpa wouldn't look Benjy in the face. As Benjy stood before the old man, he felt sorry for him. Whatever he was hiding was painful and hurting him. Benjy's anger turned to compassion and he squatted down beside the old man's rocker and pleaded, "Grandpa, answer me please. I need to know the truth."

The old man felt torn between losing his grandson for telling the truth and losing him if he didn't. Finally he stood up and walked to the screen door and opened it. Benjy thought for a minute that the old man was going to leave him there without a word, and after it was over, he wished he had done just that. But before going inside, he said, "I told you the truth a long time ago. Folks around here don't like me because they're jealous of what I've got. They can't stand it so they stay in my business, and I guess I've had to be mean to most of them. And that goes for all the do-gooders in your church. I love you, boy, but I ain't coming to your baptism." The old man's face was hard and cold, and Benjy knew he meant it. He walked into the house without another word.

Benjy didn't follow him, but he didn't let him have the last word, either. His grandpa's words had cut deep, and he was on the verge of crying. He was choking back his tears as he yelled out to the empty doorway, "You don't love me. Don't tell me that, because if you did, those other folks wouldn't matter to you. You're saying they're more important than me, and if that's the truth, I don't want you to come

135

after all!" Benjy stopped to see if the old man would reappear, but he didn't. Benjy called out once more, "Did you hear me, Grandpa, I don't want you there!" And again he waited for the old man to appear. And then as he walked away, he turned and shouted, "Maybe my papa was right about you. Maybe I should start listening to him more!"

The old man stood in the darkness of the house and watched as his grandson ran down the road.

CHAPTER SEVENTEEN

Amazing Grace

Benjy thought things would never be the same between his grandpa and him. Days went by without a word from the old man, and the time passed like a terrible nightmare. Benjy was hurting double for what he had said to his grandpa and again for what his grandpa had said to him. He wanted to go to the old man and tell him he was sorry for what had happened, but he was afraid it would just make things worse. He wasn't sure if his grandpa would ever forgive him, and it bothered him that the old man had not come to see him, either. He wanted to believe that his grandpa was hurting as much as he was, but there was no reason to think that was true.

His momma and papa didn't ask Benjy about what had happened, but they knew by his actions that it was just as they had predicted. His momma did not interfere, but it was not because she didn't want to. It was to be as his papa had said in the beginning: "If the boy sees his grandpa for a good man, then he will be seeing something the rest of us missed. And if he sees his bad side, then he will make the decision as to whether he wants to be around him or not."

Benjy did not sleep a wink on the Saturday night before his baptism. He knew he was supposed to be excited about being saved, but he wasn't because things weren't right. He talked to God that night, and as he had always done, he started making deals with Him. As Benjy saw it, he needed to ask God for a favor. He wanted his grandpa to be in church and see him get baptized, but more than that, he wanted things to be right between them again. Benjy explained that if his grandpa would come to church, maybe people would see that he really was a good man, and they would quit talking bad about him. Benjy finally went to sleep with a silent prayer in his heart.

He felt better the next morning. On their way to church, his momma and papa were trying to be cheerful to help his feelings, and it did help some. Benjy wanted to believe that his prayer would be answered, but something deep down inside of him caused him to have his doubts. As they entered the church, he searched the pews like a hawk for a glimpse of his grandpa, but he was nowhere to be seen. Benjy saw B.J. Williams on the back pew and he remembered the fight betwen them when they were in the fourth grade. Now he really wanted his grandpa to show up, just so B.J. would finally know he had been wrong about the old man. It was important to Benjy that everyone in the church know how wrong they had been about his grandpa.

They took their seats, and each time the door opened, Benjy turned around to look. If his grandpa found it in his heart to come, he would not sit alone. Benjy knew it would make his momma and papa mad, but he would sit with his grandpa no matter what.

The service started and whatever Preacher Wilson was saying, Benjy did not hear. It made him feel bad, too. He knew that the least he could do was to pay attention on the day he was to be baptized. But no matter how hard he tried, he couldn't keep his mind on anything but his grandpa. Finally his momma got tired of his turning around and she whispered in his ear, "Son, be still and pay attention. He's not coming." Her words were harsh, but Benjy knew they were true.

When Benjy heard Preacher Wilson ask if there was anybody who needed to make a profession of faith to the church and God, he almost didn't get up. He wasn't sure anymore. There were too many things wrong. He knew his mind wasn't right, and he was thinking maybe his heart wasn't, either. His papa put his arm around Benjy's shoulders and gently pushed him from his seat. Once he was on his knees and praying with Preacher Wilson, he knew again that it had been the right thing to do.

After the service, they all headed down to the river.

There were four others who were going to be baptized that day, so everybody in the church made the trip. As Benjy stood looking out across the waters of the great Arkansas River, his papa once again put his arm around him. He leaned over and whispered, "The Good Lord is with you, Benjy, and He knows your pain. I guess your grandpa is just as much a burden to God as he is to you. But you're not alone, and you never will be now."

Benjy just nodded his head and started to walk to the river's edge. His momma caught up with him and gave him a soft kiss on the cheek. Between his papa's words and his momma's kiss, Benjy was almost in tears, because he was happy and sad at the same time.

Benjy walked out into the cool water of the river and took Preacher Wilson's hand. It was like the water was washing away all his confusion, and he felt peaceful for the first time in a long time. He heard a voice inside his head and thought it was his papa's words coming back to him, but it wasn't. It was the Good Lord talking, and He was saying everything would be all right if Benjy just trusted Him.

Benjy felt Preacher Wilson's hand on his shoulder, and he knew he was talking too, but that wasn't the voice he heard. The boy looked out over the people gathered at the riverbank, and he saw his momma and papa standing there. Then he turned his head to the side, and what he saw was a moment of amazing grace. His grandpa was standing at the edge of the woods with his hat in his hand and his head bowed. Benjy didn't have time to react as Preacher Wilson laid him back in the water. But as he went under, he knew the true meaning of being saved and the faith and power of the Good Lord.

His grandpa was gone when Benjy came back up, and he looked around for just one glimpse of him. Nobody knew he had been there except Benjy and the Good Lord, and that was all that mattered. Benjy wasn't going to tell his momma and papa about it, but he couldn't help himself. He didn't know if he wanted to tell them just so they would know they had been wrong about his grandpa, or because he thought it might make a difference in how they felt about him. As they rode home, he said, "Grandpa was at the river today, and he saw me get baptized."

His momma and papa both looked at each other as though they doubted him. Then his papa said, "I didn't see him there. How do you know?"

Benjy could not hold back his smile of happiness. "I saw him standing at the edge of the woods. I told him if he loved me, he would be there, and I guess I've got my answer now."

His papa was silent for a long time, and Benjy wasn't sure if he had done the right thing by telling him. His papa's face was sad and his jaws were set tight, as though he were trying to hold something back. He turned his head and looked out the window as if he didn't want anybody to hear what he had to say. His voice was low and broken as he said, "I'm glad he was there for you today, son. That's more than he ever did for me."

CHAPTER EIGHTEEN

Now I Lay Me Down to Sleep

When Benjy turned sixteen, he started working in the woods during the summer with his papa. It didn't take but one day of hauling logs and Benjy knew he wouldn't have time for anything else like hunting and fishing. It was all he could do to drag himself to the supper table each night, and once the sun went down, Benjy was more than ready for bed.

On Saturdays he still made a special effort to go to his grandpa's house for a little fishing, but mostly just to visit. His papa let him take the truck, and it made Benjy feel all grown to whistle up Blue Jr. and then climb in on the driver's side and leave by himself. Driving the truck had become Benjy's new adventure.

But there was another reason Benjy made the trips on Saturdays, and that was because it seemed to mean more to his grandpa than ever before. The old man would be waiting in his rocker on the porch as he always did, but now he lit up like a lonely man in need of a visit when he saw his grandson pull into the drive. He would always say, "Boy, you sure look like your daddy driving up in his truck." Benjy couldn't help but wonder if the old man was really wishing it was his papa and if that wasn't the real reason he would get so excited when he saw him coming.

But even if his grandpa was wishing it were his own son, it was useless, because his papa wouldn't make the trips to see the old man. The only time they saw each other was when his grandpa would stop by the house to pick up Benjy to drive him on into town for supplies. The old man and his papa were nice to one another if they happened to meet, but it was obvious to Benjy that whatever had come between them was never going to change.

This bothered Benjy because his grandpa wasn't getting any younger, and his coughing spells were more frequent and seemed to be getting worse all the time. The first time Benjy saw one of these attacks, his grandpa nearly passed out and was having a hard time breathing. It scared Benjy and he said, "Grandpa, you need to get yourself to a doctor and get something for that coughing."

But as the old man gasped for air, he would grin

and try to ease Benjy's mind. "Boy, it ain't nothing but the cold winter air and too many smokes. Soon as spring gets here and the air warms, I'll be just fine. It ain't nothing a good day's fishing can't cure."

Benjy wanted to believe that his grandpa was right, but the closer it came to spring, the worse things got. Benjy and his grandpa didn't do much spring fishing because his grandpa wasn't up to it. The boy mentioned to his papa one day that his grandpa wasn't feeling well and his papa just said, "Don't worry about your grandpa, Benjy. He's too ornery to die." The mention of the word dying hit the boy like a bad dream on a stormy night. He hadn't thought about his grandpa's dying, and it made him aware of the fact that it was possible.

That night in bed, Benjy prayed just as hard for his grandpa as he had done for Ole Blue, hoping he would be spared another death of someone he loved. Benjy told the Good Lord how special his grandpa was to him and how he couldn't get along without him. He also mentioned that there wasn't any way to replace the old man like He had done with Ole Blue, just so He would know that it was absolutely necessary that his grandpa be spared.

Benjy knew the talk had done some good because the next day after church, he went over to his grandpa's house, and not only was the old man acting as spry as a filly, but he didn't cough one time during the visit.

As it turned out, his grandpa's feeling good was

just the calm before the storm. Two weeks later the old man took a turn for the worse. Benjy drove up to his grandpa's house and he wasn't sitting in his rocker on the porch. A sick feeling of fear came over Benjy, as though he already knew what had happened. He jumped out of the truck and started screaming his grandpa's name and searching the fields for just one glimpse of the old man.

It was a beautiful summer day, and it wasn't like his grandpa to be inside. Benjy started running through the barns and even ran halfway to the pond, but the old man was nowhere to be seen. Blue Jr. did not understand and thought Benjy was playing a game. He was barking wildly and wanted to join in, and when he caused Benjy to trip and fall, the boy hit his dog out of anger. Blue Jr. yelped in pain and his cry was like adding salt to a wide-open wound when Benjy realized what he had done. He had never hit a dog in his life, and as he knelt down and held the dog's trembling body, it brought him to his senses.

Benjy tried to think calmly as he wiped the sweat from his face. Maybe his grandpa was just napping and didn't hear him drive up. Maybe there was nothing wrong at all. He stood up and started walking back to the house. But it was no use. He could not rid himself of the gut feeling that something was wrong, and he took off running until he reached the house. This was the first time that he noticed the front door wasn't standing open like it usually was on a hot summer day. Benjy walked inside and immediately knew that his grandpa had not been up, because there weren't any smells of coffee and cooked bacon. These were his grandpa's rituals that always started a new day. Benjy also heard a low humming noise and found his grandpa had left the radio on all night, and the batteries were almost dead. This was just another sign that things were not right. His grandpa was too careful and never wasted his batteries.

Benjy slowly walked to the back of the house, fully expecting to find the old man dead in his bed. He knocked and then opened the door and whispered his grandpa's name. It was dark and even though Benjy could see his body in bed, he still didn't know if he was alive. He walked to the bed and saw that his grandpa's eyes were shut, and he shook him lightly. The old man's groans were like music to Benjy's ears. "Grandpa," he said, "what's the matter? Why ain't you up yet?"

The old man weakly answered back, "Boy, I ain't feeling worth spit today. I'm just too tired, just too tired."

Benjy raised the window shade to let some light into the room, and when he saw his grandpa's face, he knew the old man wasn't going to make it through the day. His eyes were dull and clouded over and his cheeks were hollowed out, leaving dark bags hanging under his eyes. Benjy felt of his grandpa's forehead, and it was cool and clammy, much like the feel of creek-bottom mud. The harder Benjy tried to remain calm, the more his insides churned in desperation.

146

"Grandpa, I'm going to get my papa and a doctor. You're real sick and need some help."

His grandpa reached out and grabbed Benjy's arm and held it tightly for a weak and sick man. He whispered, "Ain't no need, boy. The only thing I want you to do is sit here and talk to me." Benjy tried to pull free, but then he saw his grandpa's begging eyes and he knew he couldn't leave. The old man's gruff voice said, "I think a spot of coffee would help, but promise me you won't leave."

Benjy made the promise against his better judgment. He went to the kitchen and made the coffee, and then brought his grandpa a cup and helped him to raise up and drink it. The coffee seemed to help some, and more for Benjy's sake than his own, the old man managed a weak smile and said, "Maybe we'll do some fishing later on when I feel better." But after he said it, he started coughing, and it left him limp as a dish rag. Benjy tried once again to leave and get help, but his grandpa said, "I'm going to be all right, boy. Don't you worry about me. Just sit here and help me drink my coffee."

Benjy pulled a chair close to his grandpa's bed and sat down. The old man laid his head back, and his eyes stared at the ceiling as he began to talk about his younger days. Benjy felt a sudden fear in him worse than the thought of his grandpa dying. He thought his grandpa was ready to reveal the truth about his past, and Benjy was not sure if he was ready to hear it. It didn't seem to matter anymore. There was nothing his grandpa could say now to change the way he felt about him, and the truth would serve no purpose. Benjy got up and said, "Grandpa, you need a doctor and I have to go get you one."

He was almost to the door when his grandpa said, "Don't leave me, Benjy. I ain't wanting to die alone." The words pierced through the boy like lightning, and he was caught between running to get help and a dying man's last request. Then the old man held out his hand with those long, skinny fingers that had tickled his ribs more than once, and Benjy came back, took his hand, and sat down once again. "I'll stay, Grandpa, but you need to quit talking and save your strength."

But the old man ignored his grandson's words. "You never got to meet your grandma, and it's a shame. She was a fine woman and as pretty as a spring day." Benjy watched as the old man's cloudy eyes filled with tears and he said, "I loved that woman more than anything else in this world, and no matter what anybody else tells you when I'm gone, you remember that, boy." Benjy felt a lump the size of Texas in his throat. But before he had time to say anything, his grandpa looked at him and said, "When your grandma died, something inside of me died too, and I wasn't the same man again. I got bitter and blamed the world for losing her, and I did some things I ain't proud of now. But I've been living with them all my life, and I kept my promise to your daddy. Now it's time to let them go."

Benjy lowered his head and waited to hear the truth that had been denied him all his life. But the room remained silent. When he looked up again, the old man's eyes were closed, as though he had drifted off into a peaceful sleep. Benjy held his hand tightly, and then watched as his grandpa took a gasping breath and squeezed his hand. There was no life left in him, and there was no peace on his face as he died.

Benjy didn't panic and go running for help like he thought he would. He just sat there and cried for a long time, like a boy was supposed to do when he had just lost a man he loved so much. He cried because of the loss, and he cried because no one except him cared that the old man had passed away. He was glad he had stayed, because it was only right that he be the one to see his grandpa through his dying.

Benjy wasn't in a hurry to leave. Time didn't matter much to a dead man and the only one sorry for his death. He pulled the covers over his grandpa's head and prayed that God would have mercy on his soul. The prayer that came to mind was one that his momma had taught him to pray before bedtime. And he whispered softly, "Now I lay me down to sleep. I pray the Lord my soul to keep. If I should die before I wake, I pray the Lord my soul to take." Benjy pulled the covers back again and kissed his grandpa's forehead. He whispered, "I love you, Grandpa." And his only wish was that he had said it sooner.

Benjy loaded Blue Jr. and drove home with the awful thought that he was probably the only one who

loved his grandpa. It seemed all too real now that
the old man was dead. As he drove up to his house,
he saw his papa splitting logs out by the barn, and
his momma was sitting on the porch doing some knitting. His momma saw Benjy first, and the expression
on his face told her something was wrong. She stood
up, letting her knitting fall to the floor, and asked in
a worried voice, "Son, what's the matter? Something
bad has happened, hasn't it?"

Benjy looked at his momma and realized he didn't
want to tell her, like it wasn't any of her business.
She didn't care about the old man when he was alive,
so why should she care that he was dead? Benjy
ignored her questions and walked to the barn.

His papa stopped and mopped his brow with one
swipe of his shirtsleeve. He too, could tell by the
look on his son's face as he watched him approach
that something bad had happened, and he knew
what it was. Benjy calmly said, "Your daddy died
this afternoon in his bed." The boy had wondered
what his papa would do when the day and time
finally came, and his papa would have to face the
fact that there weren't any chances left for making
peace with his own daddy. His papa didn't reply, but
instead seated himself on his splitting stump and
leaned both arms across his ax. He stared out across
the yard, as if thinking the same thing as his son. It
was over now. Years and years of pain and lost love
filled his heart.

It was the first time in Benjy's life that he truly felt

sorry for his papa, and he wanted to hug him. But at the same time, the boy was also feeling a great deal of disappointment in his papa. If he was feeling bad for the way he had treated his own daddy all these years, he deserved it. Benjy hoped he would think about it for a long time. He turned to leave, and his momma was standing there with her hand over her mouth and a look of disbelief on her face. As he walked past her, she put her hand on his shoulder. Benjy shrugged it off and walked into the house.

He went to his bed and lay down with a picture in his mind of the both of them standing outside in their sorrow. They were not sorry because the old man had died, but sorry they had allowed him to slip away without caring anything about him. The longer Benjy lay there, the worse it ate at him, and he realized that his sadness had turned to anger. He was angry at the whole world for not having better sense and a little forgiveness for a man and his mistakes. It just wasn't right for a man to go to his grave being so disliked by his own son for some stupid mistakes he had made a long time ago. Benjy had always known his papa to be an understanding man and forgiving in his ways. It didn't make sense to the boy that he would allow his own daddy to die, alone and unloved. Benjy couldn't think of anything that his papa could do to him that would make Benjy turn against him like that.

He rolled over and tried to make all his feelings go away. There were only two things that he was sure of now. He knew that he loved his grandpa, and he knew he was a good man. Nothing was ever going to change that. He just wished that his papa had taken his own advice that he had given to his momma years ago. Because if he had taken the time, he, too, would have seen the good man that Benjy had come to know and love.

Benjy heard his papa leaving in the truck, and he knew he was going over to take care of his grandpa's body. He thought once of going with him, but then he changed his mind. It was too late, but maybe his papa was needing to spend some time with his daddy. He heard his momma open the door to his room and Benjy closed his eyes, hoping she would leave him alone. He heard her walk across the room and then felt her hand as it brushed softly through his hair. Benjy didn't move and she left the room. He wasn't ready to face her or anybody else. There wasn't anybody who really cared, anyway.

Benjy fell asleep without any supper and slept through the rest of the night. He wasn't sure whether he dreamed it or not, but sometime in the night, he looked up and saw his papa at the end of his bed with his head in his hands.

CHAPTER NINETEEN

A Legend Lives On

The next morning Benjy got up early and left without breakfast. He left a note on the table saying he had gone out to do some thinking, but the truth was, he still couldn't face his momma and papa. He and Blue Jr. started down the road, and Benjy didn't know where he was going or what he was going to do. He just needed some space and time to think.

When he found himself walking up the drive to his grandpa's house, his intentions became clear to him. He wanted to go fishing. Maybe it was because he had learned a long time ago that fishing helped to clear a troubled mind, or maybe it was because he was needing to do something that was close to his grandpa.

Benjy went to the shed and got his fishing pole. It

was the same one his grandpa had given him years ago, and it brought back the fond memories of Big Sam.

He loaded Blue Jr. in the boat. It was the first time Blue Jr. had been in the boat. But Benjy would have gladly left his dog behind for just one more chance to fish with his grandpa. Maybe fishing had not been such a good idea. There were just too many memories around the pond, and everywhere Benjy looked and everything he did reminded him of his grandpa. Even though Benjy knew his grandpa was dead, he had not accepted it yet and he didn't want to. He wasn't ready to turn loose of the old man. And that's why he was sitting in his grandpa's boat on his grandpa's pond and doing what his grandpa loved to do most.

Benjy heard the nearby hoot of an owl and quickly turned to see it perched in a tall pine on the edge of the pond. It was an unusual sight, because the owl was rarely seen in the daytime. When Benjy was younger, his grandpa told him that the owl was a mysterious bird that was all-knowing and all-seeing. It stayed hidden in the daytime and hunted at night. He said that the bird could see things in the night that no other creature had the eyes for, not even man. One night around a campfire, Coot Hunter heard the owl and told a story from an Indian legend. He said that if a man stared into the eyes of the owl, he could see both his past and his future. Benjy never believed the legend, but he wondered if there was a purpose behind the strange appearance of this owl. Could this bird see inside his heart? Did he know of the pain and confusion Benjy was feeling right now? Benjy paddled up to the bank near the pine tree and was surprised that the owl was not scared into flight. He watched the bird for a long time, and it could have been his imagination, but he really thought the eyes of the owl were staring back at him. Then all of a sudden, Benjy stood in the boat, raised two clenched fists in the air, and yelled up in desperation, "Do you have all the answers? If you're so wise, why don't you tell me the truth? Why did everybody hate my grandpa? Why did he have to die? Why do I feel so all alone?" Benjy dropped back to his seat and held his head in his hands. At first he felt foolish at his outburst, but then he started to feel some relief as he realized how good it felt to say aloud the things he was feeling on the inside. Blue Jr. started to whine, and as Benjy reached out to pet him, he looked back to the owl and it was gone.

Benjy felt lost and defeated, and he almost gave in and went back home. But when he saw Big Sam's stump, he knew what he wanted to do. He knew what he had to do. Today he would catch the legend. He had fished for him many times since the day Big Sam had gotten away and never had any luck. His grandpa told him once that it was a waste of time, because the fish had probably died of old age.

But Benjy didn't want to believe that, especially now. Trying to catch Big Sam the first time had become a special memory from his childhood days, and maybe his desire to catch the fish now was to relive that memory and make his grandpa proud of him.

Whatever the reason, Benjy was driven like he had become possessed. He paddled the boat around to the side under the willows and sat there a minute, remembering the first time he had hung Big Sam. He started to laugh as the image of his grandpa hanging between the boat and willow came to mind. He would never forget the look on the old man's face when he finally fell into the water. It all came back to him as though it had happened yesterday.

Finally Benjy threw his worm against the stump. He was leaning over the side of the boat when he saw his line go tight and start off to the right. Benjy knew it had to be Big Sam, and he let him get a good hold on the worm. Then the boy lay back and set the hook as hard as he could. Big Sam didn't waste any time yanking back, and the fight was on. Benjy would reel in a foot or so of line, and Big Sam would pull it right back out. The fish came out of the water and jumped a good two feet in the air. To Benjy, it was the prettiest sight of a fish he had ever seen. He was just as excited as the first time he had hung Big Sam, and before he knew what he was doing, he hollered out, "Did you see that, Grandpa? I got him this time! I got him good!"

And even though Benjy knew it was impossible, he thought he heard his grandpa's reply, "Get 'em, boy. Don't let him get loose." That was all the encouragement Benjy needed, and he brought Big Sam in. At first, Benjy was wild with excitement and pride for being the only person to ever catch Big Sam. As he watched that big fish lying in the bottom of the boat, he let out a whoop that could be heard for miles.

Big Sam was not as large as Benjy remembered, but the fish was still the biggest one he had ever caught. Big Sam's back was as black as a moonless night and his sides sparkled in silver. A dark, greenish stripe divided the two colors, and he had the true markings of a largemouth bass. Big Sam was as long as the paddle Benjy laid beside him and as wide as the spread of two hands. He was, indeed, the most beautiful fish Benjy had ever seen.

But then as Benjy reached down to pick the fish up, a different sort of feeling overcame him. Normally, a fish with that much fight in him would still have been flouncing and jumping for freedom. But Big Sam was just lying there gasping for air, and it was more than Benjy could take. It reminded him too much of his grandpa lying in bed, gasping for his own last breath before dying. The connection between the fish and his grandpa was too strong, and Benjy knew what he had to do. He carefully eased Big Sam over the side of the boat and said, "Live a good, long life, Sam. You deserve it."

Off in the far distance, Benjy heard the resounding call of the owl, and he smiled as he watched the fish swim away. When he saw a swirl around his stump, he knew Big Sam was home again and safe. He hoped it was the same way for his grandpa. It was the first time since his grandpa's death that he felt any peace inside him. He rubbed Blue Jr.'s head and said, "There ain't no need in two legends dying. One is all I can take in today."

CHAPTER TWENTY

The Truth

The funeral took place a couple of days later. The old man was buried in the King Cemetery beside his wife, and there weren't many folks attending. Those who were there were present to comfort his momma and papa, not to pay their last respects. Benjy didn't cry anymore, because he had done his crying beside his grandpa's bed on the day he died.

He watched his momma and papa, hoping to see some sign that they really did care. But they both just stood there and watched as the old man was lowered in the ground, and there was no change in their expressions as the preacher said meaningless words over his grave. Benjy thought about what his grandpa had said about loving his wife so much, and it comforted him some to see him finally being laid to rest beside her. It was the only good memory he would have of that day.

After the funeral, they left and went back home. A few people had been coming by the past two days to bring food and visit, but it wasn't for his grandpa's sake, so Benjy stayed off to himself. Some of the folks who had attended the funeral followed them home, and Benjy asked his papa if he could use the truck. He told him he wasn't up to visiting with anybody and just wanted to ride around. His papa said, "I know how you feel, and if you don't mind, I'd like to come along."

His papa's offer took the boy by surprise, because they had not been talking much since his grandpa died. Either there wasn't much to say, or the both of them were too uncomfortable about saying it. Benjy answered, "You're welcome to come along if you want."

They loaded Blue Jr. in the back and his papa said, "I'd like to drive, if you don't mind." Benjy agreed, and as they pulled into the drive to his grandpa's house, he knew why his papa had asked to drive. The sun was beaming down, and it was a dog-day afternoon, hot and sticky and humid. They walked up to the porch, and when Benjy saw his grandpa's rocker sitting there empty, it was all he could do to fight back the tears.

Benjy took a seat on the steps of the porch with his back to the rocker and watched as his papa took his knife and tobacco plug from his pocket and then sat down beside him. He took a cut from the plug and then offered it to his son. Benjy had been chewing some lately, but he refused the offer. He realized how uncomfortable he felt sitting there, and at first, he thought it was because it was his grandpa's porch. But then he realized the uneasiness was between him and his papa. His love for his grandpa and his papa's lack of love for the old man was as real as though it had taken a seat in the empty rocker behind them.

His papa was feeling it too, and Benjy watched as he searched the ground for a stick to whittle on with his nervous hands. He made a few cuts on a twig and then he said, "Son, I ain't expecting you to understand everything I'm about to tell you, but I've got this sore inside of me and if I don't get everything out in the open, it will never heal." Benjy had heard those exact words from his grandpa, and he wondered if his papa really knew how much alike the two men were in their thinking.

His papa said, "Maybe you should have been told this a long time ago. I made the decision not to tell you because I knew how much you loved your grandpa, and I didn't want to change that, and I still don't." His papa stopped and looked at his son as if expecting some reply, but all Benjy could do was nod.

He knew that what his papa had to say was hard for him and had caused him much pain over the years. Finally he said, "Papa, go ahead and tell me. I know it's hard for you, but I need to know."

His papa took a deep breath and looked out across the yard. "I ain't proud of what's come between me and my daddy. It happened a long time ago, and I guess it was the pain at first and then pride later on that kept us from forgiving one another. I was only ten years old when Momma died, and I had a brother who was fourteen. His name was Bartholomew, but everyone just called him Buddy."

His papa stopped to spit, and Benjy was glad for the interruption. He needed time to believe what he was hearing. He had never known about any brother, and it was like his papa was telling him some kind of bedtime story that wasn't real. Benjy said, "I didn't know you had a brother. What happened to him? Where is he now?"

His papa replied, "Buddy is a big part of why I felt the way I did about my daddy. You see, the night my momma died, my daddy was away on some kind of business. She got sick and had a fainting spell, and Buddy left me alone with her while he went to get a doctor. But she died before Buddy could get back. I was sitting right there beside her bed and I fell asleep. I didn't even hear a sound when she died. Buddy and the doctor woke me up when they came into the room, and the only thing I remember is Momma must have reached out and held my hand before she died, because she was still holding it when they came in. The doctor took one look at Momma and pulled the covers over her head and took us from the room.

"Buddy took Momma's dying real hard, and even though I knew it had happened, I didn't fully understand it. I was crying, but it was mostly because I saw Buddy so upset. You've got to understand something, Benjy. He wasn't just an ordinary brother

161

to me. He was like my idol, my best friend and my keeper, all in one. I had never loved anyone like I loved him until you came along. That's why I named you Bartholomew. It was the only name fitting for a King."

Benjy remembered back to the first grade when he had learned how to write his name. It explained why his momma had cried when she told him about his name, and it explained the sad looks on his papa's and grandpa's faces when they saw it written down on Benjy's paper. The pieces of the puzzle were beginning to fit, and Benjy asked, "So what happened to Buddy?"

The look on his papa's face was so much like the look he had seen on his grandpa's face so many times that Benjy had to turn away. His papa said, "Well, my daddy thought Buddy was to blame for Momma's dying. The doctor told him that it was her weak heart, and there wasn't anything that anyone could have done to save her. But Daddy wouldn't hear to it. He was like a madman and even took a leather strap and beat Buddy for letting his momma die. And it didn't stop after the funeral. My daddy beat my brother with that strap almost every day. Benjy, there is no way I can explain to you what it did to me to see Buddy get whipped time and time again for something he hadn't done. He would be so sore and in so much pain that he could hardly crawl into bed at night. All I could do was lay there beside him and cry for his pain.

"Buddy was a real good student in school and

everybody liked him, but even that changed. Buddy wouldn't talk to anyone and started missing school. The principal got worried and came to see Daddy, and that's when folks started finding out the truth. Daddy embarrassed Buddy in front of the principal by telling the story of how Buddy let his momma die. My brother never went back to school after that.

"Buddy got the same treatment every time someone from the church came to visit. Momma was real religious and the family never missed a Sunday in church. But Daddy stopped going once Momma died. The church folks were real faithful and kept stopping by, only to hear Daddy rant and rave about the devil in Buddy. Everybody knew it wasn't true, but if they tried to say different, Daddy would get real mad and run them off. When I was eleven and Buddy was fifteen, he finally had all he could take and he ran away."

Benjy heard his papa's voice crack, and he knew he was crying. It was the first time he had ever seen him cry, and the boy felt like a big hawk had landed on his chest and ripped his heart out. He was crying too, and wiped the tears as they ran down his cheeks. His papa's voice was full of sadness. "Benjy, I ain't never felt so much lonesome pain in my life as the day Buddy left me. I begged him to take me with him, but he said if I went, Daddy was sure to coming looking for him. But he knew if he left alone, Daddy wouldn't care, and he was right, too. The only thing Daddy said when he found out Buddy was gone was, 'Good. That's one less mouth to feed.' I ain't never forgot those words, and I guess I hated my daddy then more than ever.''

His papa stopped to spit again, and Benjy sat there with a sick feeling in the pit of his stomach and his heart was broken. He couldn't believe that his papa was talking about the same man he had known and loved so much. Finally he said, "Papa, what happened to Buddy?"

His papa cleared his throat and continued, "Well, we got a letter from the army about six months later, saying Buddy had been killed in the war. They had his name down as 'Private First Class Bartholomew King.' Daddy threw the letter away, but I snuck it out and I've still got it. It's all I have left of him.''

Benjy asked, "If Buddy's dead, how come he ain't buried in the King Cemetery? I ain't never seen his grave.''

His papa shook his head. "I guess this last part was what really turned the whole town against Daddy for good. Most folks knew about the beatings and how cruel and mean Daddy treated Buddy, and they knew Daddy was the reason Buddy ran away. But that was family matters and I guess nobody wanted to get involved. Things changed, though, when Daddy refused to let the army send his body home to be buried in our cemetery, and it brought the whole town to our doorsteps. There were people coming by night and day, madder than hell about it. They said it wasn't right. Buddy had died for his country, and he was a hero. During the war, folks were mighty patriotic. They believed if a boy went off and fought and died for his country, then he was to be treated as a hero and given the respect he deserved. They said it didn't matter what had come between Buddy and Daddy. All that mattered was that Buddy be given a proper burial and be laid to rest beside his momma. I overheard Daddy telling one man that he'd sooner die in hell as to see Buddy buried next to Momma. That man just shook his head and said, 'I guess you'll get your wish on both accounts. I just hope it's worth it to you.' The whole church congregation, carrying an American flag, showed up at our house one Sunday after church, begging Daddy to sign the papers and let Buddy come home. They said they would be responsible for the funeral and bury him in another cemetery. But Daddy just stood on these front steps we're sitting on now and grinned like justice was being served. Daddy became a terrible legend that day and folks never forgave him. Anyway, Buddy was buried in some soldier cemetery up North. Someday I'm going up there too, and see his grave. I made that promise to myself the day he died."

Silence filled the afternoon air as Benjy sat there believing the most unbelievable story he had ever heard. He knew it was true, because every little thing that had been said to him over the years now made sense. But it was still so hard to believe. He looked at his papa and said, "I know you're telling me the truth, Papa, but it's so hard to believe Grandpa did those things."

His papa said, "I know it is, son. I couldn't understand it either when I was ten years old and it was

165

happening to me, but I guess I've had plenty of years since then to try and make sense of it all. There ain't a day goes by that I don't think about it. But time doesn't help much. The only conclusion I've come to in all these years is that deep down inside, my daddy blamed himself for not being there when Momma died. He loved that woman, and I guess he would have brought her the moon if she would have asked for it. I heard it said once that when a person is hurt deep or angry at himself, he hurts those closest to him. I guess Daddy took all his pain and anger out on Buddy. But even knowing that, it doesn't make things right. Daddy had plenty of time to get over Momma's death and make amends for what he did to Buddy. He just never did it."

His papa turned and looked at Benjy. "I'd like to think that the way my daddy treated you was his own way of making up for all the bad things he did to Buddy. I told him once that if he ever said one bad word about Buddy to you, or mentioned his name, he would never see you again. I meant it too, and I guess my daddy took my word on it."

Benjy remembered what his grandpa had said before dying, and he told his papa, "Before Grandpa died he said that he had kept his promise to you. I guess that's what he was talking about."

With a nod of his head, his papa replied, "It's the only decent thing he ever did that I asked of him."

There was just one more thing Benjy needed to know, and he wasn't sure why, but it seemed important to him. "Papa, how did you really feel when you found out Grandpa had died?"

His papa sighed a heavy breath and thought for a long time before he answered the question. Then he said, "I felt sad, Benjy, real sad. But it wasn't just because he died. It was more because he died never having made amends for what he did. I guess it's a most miserable life to live, knowing you've done somebody wrong but never having the courage to admit to it. At least, he never admitted it to me. I ain't sure whether I could have forgiven my daddy for what he did to Buddy, but if he would have come to me and admitted his wrong and asked to be forgiven, I guess I would have tried. As it is, he died and I don't guess I'll ever know."

There was another question in Benjy's heart, and this time he knew why he had to ask it. "Papa, now that Grandpa's dead, do you forgive him?"

This was a question of the heart, and his papa knew it. He knew that the right answer to tell his boy was "yes," because a man should always find forgiveness in his heart. It was a part of the Lord's Prayer to forgive those who trespass against you. But at the same time, the truth was he had not yet been able to do that. He looked away from his son and gave him the only answer he knew. "I can't answer that just yet, son. I don't guess it matters much now. The way I see it, it's now between my daddy and the Good Lord. I know God is forgiving. The question is, did my daddy ever do the asking?"

His papa stood up and started to walk away. But Benjy couldn't let him leave. He stood up and called,

"Papa, there's something I want to tell you." His papa stopped and turned around to face Benjy. "I'm proud of my name and I thank you for giving it to me. And when you make that trip up North to visit Buddy's grave, I'd like to come with you." His papa smiled, but before he could say anything, Benjy said, "I also want you to know that I'm glad you gave me a chance to get to know my grandpa. I don't like my grandpa for all the bad things he did to you and Buddy, but I still love him for all the good things he did for me. Maybe Grandpa did treat me the way he did to make up for all the wrong he had done. But he couldn't have done it unless you gave him the chance."

Benjy stopped for a moment as he discovered the most important truth. Then he said, "You said you couldn't answer me about whether you had forgiven your daddy or not. But I think deep down inside you forgave him the day you let him become a part of my life."

His papa's arms held him tightly, but another voice had begun to speak. It was his grandpa's, and the words were from a very special memory. A long time ago when Benjy confided in his grandpa about being dumb, his grandpa's reply had been, "Boy, you ain't dumb. You figure things out that a grown man spends a lifetime trying to learn."

It was like the early morning fog lifting from a quiet pond. Benjy's heart was still as he realized two truths were being revealed. One was about his grandpa, and the other was about himself.